DATE DUE

I've travelled the world twice over,
Met the famous: saints and sinners,
Poets and artists, kings and queens,
Old stars and hopeful beginners,
I've been where no-one's been before,
Learned secrets from writers and cooks
All with one library ticket
To the wonderful world of books.

© JANICE JAMES.

RAINBOW'S END

The sleepy village of Middlehope is suddenly jerked into life by the arrival of nouveau riche antiques magnate Arthur Rainbow. But the Middlehope community rejects him, and when Rainbow's crushed body is found in the graveyard of St Eata's church, there is little surprise or sorrow — but much speculation. After all, there are so many candidates — his young wife, the usurped organist, the mutinous choir. It falls upon Superintendent George Felse, newly promoted head of the Midshire CID, to solve this most perplexing murder.

ELLIS PETERS

RAINBOW'S END

Complete and Unabridged

ULVERSCROFT
Leicester

First published in Great Britain in 1978 by
Macmillan & Company Limited
London

First Large Print Edition
published October 1992
by arrangement with
Macdonald & Co. (Publishers) Limited
London

British Library CIP Data

Peters, Ellis
    Rainbow's end.—Large print ed.—
Ulverscroft large print series: mystery
I. Title
823.914 [F]

    ISBN 0–7089–2733–5

Published by
F. A. Thorpe (Publishing) Ltd.
Anstey, Leicestershire
Set by Words & Graphics Ltd.
Anstey, Leicestershire
Printed and bound in Great Britain by
T. J. Press (Padstow) Ltd., Padstow, Cornwall

1

THE gate-posts, until recently shorn of their crests and leaning drunkenly out of true, now stood up regally on either side of the drive, crowned with a pair of baronial lions, gripping in their paws escutcheons certainly not native either to the building, which was in fact a rather monstrous eighteenth-century vicarage, built by a wealthy pluralist in the days when such remote parishes carried a stipend fit for a prince, or the present owner, who was a come-lately antique dealer from Birmingham, the first landlord since 1800 to be able to duplicate the founder's extravagant fancies. No doubt the lions had been acquired in the course of business, but they looked sufficiently imposing, looming whitely in the early September dusk between dark-rose brick, and backed by clipped, cavern-dark cypresses. And hadn't the gate-posts themselves been upped by a couple of feet, to tower so high above George Felse's Volkswagen as he drove in? It was a fair preparation for what was to come.

The drive was newly-surfaced, the grass on either side shorn like a second-year lamb. Nicely-spaced cypresses accompanied the traveller, with the occasional life-size nymph or satyr, possibly marble, probably lead, posed against their darkness in antique pallor. Posed, as George noted, very tastefully, every dimension studied as meticulously as if this remote upper end of Middlehope, the rim of the world between England and Wales in these parts, had been the serene preserve of Stourhead, in Wiltshire, the final perfection of the landscape garden in these islands. Every tree placed with care, every vista calculated with the precision of a master-photographer, every view not so much an accident of nature as a dramatic composition. Between the trees sudden blazons of flowers shone in noble golds and burnished bronzes, like flares lit in the cradling dark.

"How long did you say he'd been installed here?" asked Bunty dubiously, hunching her right shoulder against her husband's left, like a loyal colleague in a battle-line closing ranks.

"Three months. Oh, I've no doubt most of these garden-gods were lying around here, it was that sort of set-up once before. Either flat on their faces or breast-deep in grass and shrubs. It wouldn't take so long to get them set up again. And from all accounts he's got the money to indulge his fancy. They'll be glad of the jobs, they're hanging on by their teeth here, the older ones. The kids head on out, more's the pity. He could be a blessing if he employs local labour."

"He knows his stuff," admitted Bunty, gazing wide-eyed at the Psyches and Graces flickering by. Bunty knew hers, though her field was music rather than landscaping, and could appreciate authority when it showed. So why wasn't she happy? Three months isn't very long, and the extreme head of a valley climbing over frontier hills from England into Wales is hypersensitive territory, critical and aloof, resentful of mere mechanical aids like expertise.

"In several fields, apparently," said George drily. "And does his homework, too." For one of the newcomer's interests was also music, and he had arrived already primed with the knowledge that Bernarda Elliot, once a promising mezzo-soprano with a bright future before her, was one and the same with Bunty Felse, long since dwindled into a wife, and to the newly-promoted head of the Midshire C.I.D. of all people. The sole reason they had been invited to this house-warming, according to Bunty, was because she had let herself be conned into acting as secretary to the Comerbourne Musical Association, and their host showed every sign of planning a takeover bid for that earnest body, and was recruiting support at every opportunity.

"I know I got myself into this," admitted Bunty frankly. "But you could easily have got out of it if you'd wanted to. I wonder why you didn't?"

"Curiosity, mainly. It pays to take a close look at every major development in these parts." He didn't go into details, there was no need. The remorseless waves of urbanisation had rippled outwards from the lowlands into the ramparts of Middlehope, and reached as far as Mottisham, which was the halfway mark, but Abbot's Bale and the scattered hill-farms round it remained a fortress of tribal solidarity. Lucky valley, still viable for a limited population, owing to sheep farming and small personal craft industries, beautiful enough and just near enough to more populated centres to attract those commuters most grimly determined on peace and rural society, while remote enough to discourage the merely rich and pretentious. By no means a closed community, it had assimilated a number of retiring, and retired, artists and academics, and tolerated a few suburban hangers-on, who, given the atmosphere, would either adapt, or lose heart and sell out to more congenial arrivals. Middlehope was expert in providing the atmosphere, though it condemned no one on sight. At any given moment there might be three or four newcomers on probation, of whom one or two would survive to become initiates. Not always the most obviously inoffensive candidates, either.

"Is he really good?" asked George curiously.

"Musically? Yes, very. I don't think he'd waste time on anything at which he couldn't excel."

"Or stop short of a takeover in anything at which he can excel?"

"It's early days yet to judge." They were just turning a curve in the drive, so screened with bushes that the view beyond should spring upon them with instant effect; and there, foursquare and arrogant and large in the afterglow, was the house itself, once the Old Rectory, now Abbot's Bale House, a great sweep of russet gravel before it, already stippled with the sharp colours of cars, and backed by a rise of two terraces, sporting new terracotta vases along their balustrades. "It has got a lord of the manor look about it, hasn't it?" said Bunty dubiously. "He must have unloaded quite a lot of money to get all this done in the time. He's rather committed himself, hasn't he, with a stake like that ploughed into the property?"

"Investment. He expects a set-up like this to sell antiques for him more effectively than any town shop, and it probably will."

They were approaching the open space under the terraces, where the old, blocked-up portal glared darkly from the centre of the heavily-pillared undercroft. "You remember what this place used to be, five years or so ago?" asked George, as he slid the Volkswagen neatly into line beside Willie Swayne's ancient Land-Rover. "A special school for delinquents with abnormally high IQs. One of those gallant experiments we used to float on waves of good intentions, forgetting how much they were going to cost. It couldn't hope to last long, but it went the length of ten years before the county finally gave in and acknowledged it couldn't be kept going. One or two of my brightest first-offenders landed up here. There were enough idealists to provide the kind of advanced education to keep them interested and out of mischief. More or less, anyhow! Some of them did the place credit in the end. The bright get so abysmally bored when there's nothing tough enough to stretch them."

"I bet it didn't look like this then," said Bunty, eyeing the massed flowers along the balustrades as she got out of the car.

"No. the spending was rather on personnel. It was plain living and very high thinking. The place has been derelict for want of a buyer ever since the school folded." He looked along the array of cars, many of them known to him. "It looks as if everyone who is anyone is here."

"Yes." said Bunty simply. "They would be." She did not add that Arthur Everard Rainbow had joined the Golf Club, the Arts Association, the Angling Society, and every other body that contained important people among its members, and if he could have got the entry to a club of which God was a member he would undoubtedly have invited God to his house-warming. They were about to play a small part in a very ambitious public-relations exercise. But she was not yet sure how fair she was being to Rainbow. After all, the very best of men might show as over-anxious to be accepted, in the circumstances. Give him the benefit of the doubt until all doubt was at an end. "Here we go, then," said Bunty. shaking out her long skirt and patting her short chestnut hair into order. At forty-seven she could still look thirty. "Let's go and see what he's done to the interior."

Broad, curving staircases, gleaming whitely where new stone had been inserted to make good the dilapidations of time, swept round from either end of the terraces, and brought them to the huge, wide-open double doors of the house, where noise and light gushed out to meet them. There is no other sound quite like that of a large and widely-assorted party which has not yet imbibed enough alcohol to shake its inhibitions and get off the ground. A loud but slightly wary noise, of many voices dutifully making conversation, pitched slightly higher than normally, and curiously blended, some conversations loose and easy with old friends, others tight and superficial, weighing up new acquaintances. At this stage parties are hard work. George was not looking forward to contributing very much. He might, on the other hand, learn quite a lot. He was, after all, only an adjunct of Bunty here. Whatever his ambitions, Rainbow wasn't aiming to join the police!

They stepped into a grandiose cube of a hall that went up two storeys, with a double staircase and a large gallery at its inner face, and musicians in the gallery, playing not tea-dance trifles or modern mood-music, but Vivaldi. The nearest few of a mobile and congested gathering turned heads to look at them, and a man in a polo-necked silk shirt and lightweight pale grey suit, with a black cummerbund, bore down on them instantly with cries of pleasure. The get-up was so polite and adaptable, so nicely calculated to be all things to all men, that Bunty suffered a shock of revulsion for which there was no logical reason. Poor Saint Paul! Kipling was right, it must be hell to mislay one's self, not to be anyone in the effort to be everyone.

He was about George's age, which was not far off fifty, and very much George's build, rangily made, carrying too little weight rather than too much. He had a long, narrow head, and elongated, somewhat severe features that wore his broad, welcoming smile like a mask, framed fashionably in dark, greying, abundant hair that swayed in disciplined waves to his nape, and there curved to a halt in the most discreet line possible. And to offset this mildly ascetic appearance, he had a large, hearty voice.

"Mrs Felse!" he cried. "I'm so glad you could spare an evening for us. I'm only too well aware that you know everybody here much better than I do — well, there could be a few of my own fraternity around, you'll discover them as you circulate. But here I'm in your home territory, and very glad to be."

"Nice to see the old house coming to life again," said George noncommittally. "You've done wonders with it."

"You like the results? You must look round the whole interior, everything's open tonight. A man likes to have his efforts appreciated. We made slides, you know, of the entire house and grounds — before and after. We'll have a show of them later on, if people are interested. Now, would you like to keep your stole,

Mrs Felse? I think you'll find it rather warm in here. My wife will take care of you . . . "

He looked round, mildly displeased not to find her at his elbow, and swept a commanding glance round the crowded room. "Ah, there you are, Barbara! I think you haven't yet met Mrs Felse — and Superintendent Felse, our new C.I.D. chief . . . "

There indeed she was, sweeping down upon them from a corner of the room with a long, graceful stride, leaving a scented, swirling wake behind her, like the wind through a field of corn and poppies, and drawing along after her, as if in the same impetuous breeze, no less than three bemused men, even the oldest and staidest of whom followed her several paces before he came to rest. The other two, younger and even more dazed, were swept half across the room before they span aside, one either way, and melted into new groupings and new conversations, reluctantly but resignedly. George knew neither of them, which meant that they did not belong in these

12

parts. They had the half-patronising, half-apprehensive look of strays from the city, and their clothes were just one degree too far removed from the casual valley norm. One was dark and one was fair, and both were in pursuit, how seriously there was no telling, of Barbara Rainbow. And no wonder! Clearly Rainbow was well aware of it, and that had not been the circumstance that displeased him. Probably he enjoyed having one of his loveliest possessions admired and coveted. Possibly he also found it useful?

She couldn't have been more than twenty-seven or twenty-eight, twenty years younger than her husband. She was tall and slender, almost lean, and as dark and bright as Carmen, with glittering, iris-shadowed eyes, and a mane of thick dark curls that cascaded down to her shoulders, and stopped short there in a pruned thicket of thorns, formidable as the briar hedge about the Sleeping Beauty. A straight, fierce nose and a wide, dark-red mouth that smiled with a slow assured ferocity. Very beautiful, very expensive, and probably worth every penny. The gypsy type, in modern, sophisticated gypsy clothes, a long, billowing skirt built in three tiers, in three different shades of red and three different flower-prints; a black, embroidered blouse that spilled low to leave her shoulders bare, and half her high breasts into the bargain, while shrouding her arms to just below the elbow. A lot of beads, heavy, tangled and bright, a lot of bangles in a dozen colours. And what looked like a new dishcloth twined round her hips and knotted on the left. When her feet showed as she strode, they were seen to be bare, but for some sinuous patterns in henna, and scarlet nail-varnish. She was well-named Barbara, everything about her was barbed.

But her voice, when she greeted them, was young, fresh and deep. very pleasantly pitched. "Hullo, you're Bunty, aren't you? And — George, if I may call you that? I've been talking to a lot of people who know you, you see. I'm Barbara!"

* * *

14

"Whew!" breathed Bunty, clutching a pink gin and gazing after the mane of blue-black hair as it surged away into the crowd. "Isn't that something?"

"A sales aid?" wondered George as softly. "Or an *objet d'art* for sale?"

"The Laird of Cockpen," said Bunty. "'He wanted a wife, his braw house to keep.' And 'down by the dyke-side a lady did dwell, at his table-heid he thought would look well'."

"Oh, sure! But McLeish's ae daughter turned the offer down! What did *she* want? What has *she* got out of it?"

"Look round you," said Bunty. "Now I suppose we'd better circulate, hadn't we?"

"Left or right for you?" asked George obligingly.

"You know me, always inclined left. I'll see you round the other side."

The noble hall and the reception rooms on either side, one of which housed the bar, the other the buffet, were very tastefully arranged, and adorned with so many, but so cleverly disposed, pieces of furniture, pictures, ornaments, that George found himself wondering which of them were for sale, and trying to fit them out with prices. The whole house was a show-case. A dealer living in it might well get carried away, and find at night that he'd sold the bridal bed from under himself and his wife by mistake. There were fine displays of flowers, too. The work of the gardeners, of the exotic but effective Mrs Rainbow, or of some florist from Comerbourne?

George's progress round this gallery was marked by a series of halts and exchanges with people he knew, some of them natives of this remote valley-head, others from down the valley at Mottisham, or beyond, in his own village of Comerford, or the county town itself. Everyone who was anyone had been dra   n. Not, of course, Sergeant Moon, the resident police-god of Middlehope, who was invincibly plebeian and had no obvious favours to grant, but who nevertheless would know everything that had gone on in this house by tomorrow morning. Not the innkeeper, or the few tradesmen, or the sheep-farmers. The absentees were as significant as those present.

16

★ ★ ★

"I've made up my mind," pronounced Miss de la Pole with finality, "and clinched it by telling young Stephen in front of about seven interested witnesses. I've been putting it off for months, but now there's no putting it off any longer. I shall have to resign, and he may as well take the word for the deed. Nobody knows better than I do that I've been fluffing half the notes for the past six weeks, and if the choir can tolerate it, I can't. You can argue for so long with arthritis, but it's going to have the last word in the end. Look at these finger joints!"

"They appear," said George mildly, "to be retaining a very fine grip on that whisky glass, if I may say so."

"You may! When I lose that knack, they'll be practising the anthem for my funeral. But the church's music is another matter. I won't be a drag on it any longer, I'm getting out now. After all, there's Evan, years younger than I am, and just as good — better now I'm acknowledging I'm crippled."

She looked unequivocally alert, competent

17

and masterful, as she always had and always would, a tall, erect, slender old lady with the steely, delicate profile of a Renaissance Italian, say one of the pleasanter Malatestas of Rimini. From which obscure branch of the de la Pole family she drew her ancestry nobody quite knew, and she herself had never shown any disposition to enquire, but there was no mistaking the quality. Rainbow would have bought her without pedigree, so plainly was she the genuine article. She had been organist and choirmistress at St Eata's church for thirty years, and to contemplate her departure was nothing short of revolutionary. But the thin hands that retained the significant beauty of tools well-used were certainly growing daily more deformed at the joints.

"For general use," she remarked critically, flexing the hand not employed with the glass, "they'll serve years yet. But music is music. No making do with that. I was saying so to Bunty a while ago."

"They'll be out of their minds," said George with conviction, "if they don't co-opt you as consultant for life. Somebody else can pound the keys and operate the stops no reason why you shouldn't do the office of guardian angel, is there?"

"Oh, Evan will let me interfere," she agreed serenely. "We've known each other a long time, and anyhow, we'd both feel deprived if we couldn't wrangle over everything as usual. I don't expect any problems there. After all, we've both had our work cut out, trying to restrain Stephen from chucking out all the old chants that everybody knows, and curb his enthusiasm for all these modern gobbledegook Bible versions. Such abysmal doggerel! Where do these people learn their *English*?"

"I know just what you mean," agreed George ruefully, thinking of the intoxicatingly lofty prose of Bible and prayer-book on which he had been reared. On the brink of his half-century he could still thrill to the noble cadences, when half the doctrine had been rendered suspect; and certainly no new, debased, cosy popular version was going to do anything but put him off totally.

"Our host, by the way," remarked Miss de la Pole, "is quite astonishingly competent technically on almost any keyboard instrument you could offer him. He has such a superb piano in the next room that I suspect he's going to demonstrate soon."

"So Bunty warned me," agreed George. "And she shares your opinion of his powers, if that's anything."

"Oh, yes. I'm sure we'd agree about his proficiency," said Miss de la Pole, sipping her whisky, which looked, and probably was, neat. "What a pity he isn't in the least degree musical," she added absently, smiled briefly and brilliantly at George, and sailed into the centre of the now lubricated mob towards an old acquaintance. Her formal black dress, high-necked and long-sleeved, was by no means mourning black, but high fashion, and the back view of her silver-steel hair-do had the sheen of a war-helm and the floating bravado of its crowning plume.

★ ★ ★

A light hand slapped down on George's shoulder, and a young voice, nicely balanced between impudence and shyness.

20

said in his ear: "The old place has come down in the world since our day, don't you think? Sad to see it going down the nick like this!"

George turned to look at the boy addressing him with such elaborate social assurance, and met two large, guileless blue eyes that stared him out steadily, waiting with confidence to be recognised. It took half a minute to run him to earth. Eighteen or nineteen now, by the look of him, claiming acquaintance both with George and with this house. Thick brown hair, a nice athletic build, double-jointed movements, and all the engaging cheek in the world. And who else would walk in uninvited on Rainbow's house-warming, wearing jeans and a tee-shirt with a respectable blazer, the latter probably borrowed?

"Toby Malcolm!" said George, delighted, and saw his own pleasure mirrored in the blue eyes. "Well, this is a surprise! How on earth did you manage to turn up here?"

"I didn't break and enter," said the youth buoyantly, "not this time. Not even gatecrash, really. We're playing in

Presteigne this week, so I blew over to see Sam and Jenny, and they brought me along with them."

"And you're staying overnight? Not driving tonight? Then come and get a drink, and I'll make this one do, and we'll join your folks." And when Toby was duly charged, this time, as he again remarked without embarrassment, not with breaking and entering: "What do we drink to? Success to crime?"

"From your point of view, or mine?" retorted Toby. "No, that was all kid's stuff. There are much more exciting things going on now. Come on, let's find Sam, he'll love seeing us together like this. Jenny still worries about me a bit, bless her, that's why I always come over on the old bike when we're anywhere within reach." And he plunged ahead, weaving through the babel like a quicksilver lizard, and George coasted in his wake to where Sam and Jenny Jarvis were ensconced in a safe corner.

They were not really Toby's folks, of course, unless by right of capture. He had a perfectly sound father of his own, and wealthy into the bargain, a merchant who did a lot of trading to the Middle East, and was probably somewhere out there now with his third wife, Toby's second and charming but far too young stepmother. But Sam Jarvis had taught him Latin and English and European literature in this house when it was a special school, and Toby its star delinquent, with the longest record of adventurous crime in the book, and possibly the least harmful. A brilliant cracksman at thirteen, partly out of boredom, partly out of sheer necessity to experiment with his own powers, he had never been known to lift anything more than derisory trifles in all his exploits, just to prove he had really been where he said he had been, and he had never hurt anyone, except, on occasions, himself. Sam Jarvis and his wife had chosen to remain in Middlehope when the school closed, with their one son and their prodigious library, and Sam made a living, nobody knew how good or bad, by writing textbooks and works on education. George had never needed much assurance that Toby would prove one of the world's assets in the end.

The very fact that he hared back here at every opportunity to reassure Jenny was reassurance enough for George, too.

"Here he is!" proclaimed Toby, clarion-voiced, homing in on his elders with huge satisfaction. "The gaffer who put me away! But for Mr Felse you'd never have had the pleasure of my acquaintance, think of that!"

They were as pleased as he had known they would be. Sam was a large, clumsy, shy man with a simple face and a complex mind, clean-shaven, rosy and benign. Jenny was small and svelte and dark, possessed of a natural style that did wonders for mail-order clothes. They were both as proud of Toby as of their own single offspring, and showed it a good deal more openly, since he was not really theirs.

"And what have you done with Bossie tonight?" asked George. Bossie was James Boswell Jarvis, the one shoot of this promising stem, and approaching thirteen years old. "Heaven knows you couldn't wish a baby-sitter on him, not without risk to life and limb, but I'll bet there's some sort of Praetorian guard hovering.

How do you get round it?"

"What can you do with an egghead like Bossie?" demanded Jenny, between resignation and complacency. "Sylvia Thomas comes in as *his* guest, and plays him game after game of chess until we get home. Mostly he wins, but sometimes he gives her a game out of chivalry. He's a bit sweet on Sylvia." Sylvia Thomas was a farmer's daughter, eighteen and very pretty.

"He'd have to be," agreed Toby positively, "or he'd mow her down in half a dozen moves."

"And what are you doing, these days?" George wanted to know. "Playing, you said, but you haven't said what or who. And as far as I can gather, it's something that keeps you on the move."

"Oh, sorry, I forgot you couldn't very well know about it. Thespis, that's us! We're a travelling theatre. We've got three wagons that put together into a rather ramshackle auditorium, but mostly we like to play outdoors, little festivals, all that sort of thing, and improvise according to what ground we can get. There's seven of us to

25

do everything. I'm general dog's-body on lights, staging, scenery, whatever comes along, and sometimes I play, too. Mostly I do the adaptations, to get by with so few of us. Schools, as well. It's all grist. After all, that's where I got the bug." And he beamed upon Sam with so much satisfaction that George felt himself partaking of his friend's justification. "I write plays for us, too. Bursting with social criticism, as if you wouldn't guess! But funny, too, I hope. Blame Sam — I've gone legit!"

And blessedly, that was the plain truth. There went one danger to society, rapturously transmuted into a danger to nothing more precious than the establishment, which is quite a different thing. And funny, too! Nineteen, not yet out of the bud. George moved on dutifully to his next encounter, much encouraged. The only adverse note was Toby's last remark, as he looked round the furious animation and expensive furnishing of the hall, and wrinkled his straight, fastidious nose, and knotted his mobile and mischievous mouth in a grimace of distaste at so artful a display of taste.

"It does seem a pity," said Toby with detached regret. "We had some good times here. Nobody ever really *minded* us."

★ ★ ★

George found himself brought up by a tide in the restless sea of the hall, close behind a pair of tweed-clad shoulders that topped his own by at least two inches, spare, wide and straight, carrying practically nothing but bone and sinew and leathery hide, and topped by a tall brown neck and bleached, straw-coloured head. The tweed jacket smelled of resin, fungus-bearing woodland, and late summer greenery. The head was reared and still, braced like a pointer on a spot across the hall, where Barbara Rainbow had just appeared, newly-primed glass in hand, and bare shoulders shaken free for the moment of all close attendance. In a crowded room she looked alone, however briefly, and it so happened that she was looking about her with the mane-tossing challenge of a lion — sex was irrelevant! — who has just shaken off the hunt.

From the anteroom behind her rose the first notes of a Chopin study. Rainbow was indeed demonstrating his abilities, and yes, Miss de la Pole had been right, the piano was splendid. Traffic in the hall thinned somewhat, as dutiful devotees flocked quietly towards the music. Barbara stretched and straightened and breathed deep, and looked about her with relaxed interest, assured of where her husband would be for the next quarter of an hour or so.

"Hullo, William," said George into a sun-tanned, leathery ear. "I didn't know you went in for parties."

"Hullo, George," responded Willie Swayne, with a brief but amiable smile, and returned his gaze at once to the sophisticated Romany across the room. "I don't."

"Or got invited to them, these days," added George. Plenty of people had tried it in the past, but it didn't take long to discover that William Swayne, known to the whole valley as Willie the Twig by reason of his solitary lordship of some ten square miles of new and old afforestation along the border, found nothing interesting in gatherings for social chit-chat, and preferred his deer and his setters to more garrulous company.

"Oh, yes, everybody was invited this time, even me. 'Forest warden' sounds pleasantly feudal, and who knows, he may want a haunch of venison some day." Part of Willie the Twig's forest was plantation only a few years old, but part of it was very old indeed, and had supplied venison to kings of England ever since Edward III. "I just blew in out of curiosity, I've only met the fellow once. I thought I'd have a look round, and be civil, and then shove off to the 'Gun Dog' for a pint." Judging by the distrait tone of his voice and the steady stare of his light, bright grey eyes this original plan was in process of being modified. And at that very moment Barbara Rainbow's roving gaze had lighted upon him, and very thoughtfully halted there. George felt the slight, silent tensing of sinews, the almost imperceptible leaning forward, as when a pointer is about to surge out of his concentrated immobility into action.

"I shouldn't, if I were you," said George benignly.

"On the contrary," said Willie the Twig, "being you, of course you wouldn't, but if you were me you certainly would." And without further waste of time he strode across the room, swerving only sufficiently to clear such persons and objects as got in his way, and made straight for Barbara. Who, George observed before he drifted towards his next encounter, was neither surprised nor displeased, but stood and waited, reeling in on the dark and glittering thread of her glance the only fish that had so far engaged her interest, in all these hundred or so milling about her.

"Hullo!" said Barbara. "I've been noticing you for some time, and nobody's told me who you are. I was wondering when you'd work your way round to me."

"I don't work my way round," said Willie the Twig. "I go straight across. And my name's Will Swayne. Warden of Middlehope Forest. I don't know if you like forests?"

"I never really met one," said Barbara.

Her voice was low, deliberate and thoughtful. "On closer acquaintance I think I might get to like them very much."

★ ★ ★

By the time the musical interlude ended, George had reached a little group gathered at an open window. Courteously silent until that moment, they fell into easy conversation after Rainbow had received his due acclaim. Two of them George knew well, Robert Macsen-Martel from Mottisham Abbey, down the valley, and his wife Dinah. Their half-ruinous property was in process of renovation under the guidance of the National Trust, and archaeological interest in the new acquisition was proving unexpectedly lively.

"I don't think you've met Charles Goddard," said Robert, attenuated and lank and fair. "He's advising on the work, we've been uncovering some rather good tiled floors." He was a little deprecating about saying 'we' now that he had agreed to surrender the place, but obviously he must be ploughing everything that was left of his family patrimony into endowing it, or the Trust would never have been able to accept the burden, however desirable. Robert worked in an estate office selling small new houses, in one of which he and his wife lived, and there was nothing left of the centuries of Macsen-Martels and their outworn glory except the decency and integrity contained within this desiccated and aloof exterior. Unless, perhaps, Dinah's dress, loose from the shoulders, had been chosen for more reasons than fashion? Dinah was petite, rounded and dark, born into the ranks of honest toil, and with both small feet planted firmly on the ground, and what those two apparently incompatible and wildly devoted people would produce between them gave room for interested speculation. What was more, Dinah had already detected the brief glance at her waistline, and was staring George out in sparkling silence, challenging him to ask or comment. Probably Bunty had already got all the answers.

Charles Goddard was large, impressive and grey, the silver of early distinction rather than encroaching age. He had the slightly waxen and heavy smoothness of the legal profession.

"And here's John Stubbs, who's taken over as man-on-the-spot. Someone has to live on the premises, and John's brave enough to inhabit the lodge alone, ghosts or no ghosts, and look after the whole place."

This one was younger, dark, solid and taciturn, even dour. Perhaps partly because, while he murmured his perfunctory greeting, his real attention was concentrated upon a distant corner of the room, where Barbara Rainbow and Willie the Twig were perceptibly getting on rather well together. And now George realised that both these young men he was confronting had already caught his attention once this evening. They were the two who had been drawn half across the hall in bemused pursuit of Rainbow's spectacular wife, like helpless sparks in the tail of a comet.

" — and Colin Barron, who's been an enormous help to me over a number of things I never realised were valuable assets until he briefed me. I owe Colin's acquaintance to our host, as a matter of fact, and I'm grateful. I know absolutely nothing about the antiques market," owned Robert. "It's salutary to discover that what you've been writing off as junk can realise a lot of money elsewhere, and be hailed as treasure."

This was the fair one, who belonged on sight to Rainbow's world. He was tall, and built like an athlete, but his features were urban and shrewd, his clothes, while tactfully unobtrusive, of the city and the fashion.

"I've been a friend and rival of Arthur's for a long time," he said with an amiable but knowing smile, "and learned a lot from him. Enough to know that any hare he starts is well worth coursing. When a chap like Arthur moves up into these parts, it pays to take a look at the territory and see what drew him there. I haven't caught up with the real attraction yet, I suspect, but I did discover Mottisham Abbey. In time to be useful to Mr Macsen-Martel, maybe, but you may be sure it didn't do me any harm, either. I like to be candid about it."

"I'm afraid we've been talking shop,

even on this occasion," said Robert apologetically. "My fault, I don't seem able to think of anything else at the moment. It really has become very interesting. Several schools and clubs have come into the act, and been doing splendid work, under Charles's guidance. I never imagined there'd be so much enthusiasm. We're being asked to allow party visits from so many bodies that we're planning on beginning in a few weeks. Afternoons only, and while the work's in progress they'll have to be strictly guided tours, it would be too chaotic to have people straying everywhere among the plant and materials lying around there. You wouldn't like to volunteer as a guide, would you, George? We're open to offers!"

"I doubt if I should be much of an asset," said George. "I could certainly improvise a stunning scenario for you, but the facts might cause less trouble. You seem to have recruited several competent candidates already. And there's always Professor Joyce, if you can lure him away from his magnum opus."

That was a joke strictly for local people,

who were all well aware that Professor Emeritus Evan Joyce, happily retired at sixty-odd to a decrepit but spacious cottage up the valley with his books, was busily engaged in not writing his long-projected history of Goliard poets, and almost any distraction was enough to justify him in never getting it beyond the note stage.

"I think he'd rather reserve his options at the moment," said Dinah, dimpling. "Haven't you run into him tonight? He is here. Miss de la Pole has just told him she's made up her mind to retire, and has broken the news to the vicar. We could lure him away from his Latin poets, all right, but we can't compete with the organ and the choir, not a hope. He's been waiting to get his hands on them for years."

★ ★ ★

The Reverend Stephen Baines was young, earnest and good-looking, and as poor as his eighteenth-century predecessors here had been rich. He lived in a small bungalow, a bashful bachelor looked after by a widowed neighbour who cooked and cleaned, and nursed selective match-making plans for him, taking her time about both choice and tactics. He was as unaware of this as he was of many other practical proceedings that went on round him. He had some distressing proclivities, according to his parishioners, who were protectively fond of him none the less. He worried about the church's image, and tended to try all sorts of new gimmicks to get nearer to people who felt, as it happened, very close indeed, the gimmicks notwithstanding. He was given to trying out new texts in the vernacular, and adopting attitudes which were hard work for him and a great trial to his long-suffering aides. Luckily he was sound on music, which he loved.

"Isn't it lucky," he said happily, "that there should be someone so able, just coming into our community at the very time when he's needed? Providential, you might almost say. Indeed, I feel sure Mr Rainbow is going to prove a great asset in every way. We shall miss our dear de la Pole, how could we not? She's such a stalwart, and has such a way with the boys. But they sometimes need a firm hand, you know, and then, Mr Rainbow is really an outstanding musician. I can hardly believe he's really agreed to take over as organist and choirmaster. Do you know, he even volunteered? Such a busy chap, and yet willing to take on this further work in addition to everything else. And he's offered his house and grounds for the harvest supper, too."

"Most generous!" said George hollowly. What can you say. There was Evan Joyce across the room, talking to Bunty, unkempt, shaggy and endearing in his rusty black suit that must have served him for every formal occasion since his graduation, and here was this exasperating innocent who had just given away what Evan wanted most in this small chosen world of his, to a stranger, and one who showed signs of appropriating this, literally, in addition to everything else.

"Isn't it? He even intimated that he would be delighted to serve as churchwarden if there should be a vacancy. Willing workers are not so thick on the ground these days."

This one, thought George resignedly as

he moved on to confront the deprived professor and reclaim Bunty, shows every sign of being very thick on the ground indeed. A walking takeover bid for Middlehope, where he seemed to think there was a vacancy for a squire, if not a lord of the manor. He couldn't be expected to know in advance that 'squire' was a dirty word in these tribal regions. But very, very soon someone would have to start instructing him.

★ ★ ★

They foregathered in the saloon bar of the 'Gun Dog' afterwards, for one social drink together before they scattered for home: George and Bunty, Evan Joyce, Sam and Toby Malcolm (Jenny having gone straight home to relieve Sylvia Thomas of her watch), Miss de la Pole, and Willie the Twig, who came late and was unusually thoughtful and quiet. They talked about the weather, and the harvest prospects, and the forthcoming Flower and Vegetable Show, and the sad fact that the 'Gun Dog' was not a home-brewed house, like the 'Sitting

Duck' at Mottisham. But never a word about Rainbow. Not until Miss de la Pole drained her glass and rose to set a good example, drawing her black shawl round her shoulders.

"He won't do, you know," she said with inexorable gentleness; and having pronounced her oracle, as gently and decidedly withdrew, leaving them room either for comment or for silence.

As it turned out, no one had anything to object, or to add.

2

SERGEANT JACK MOON lived
one short remove from the village
of Abbot's Bale, down the valley,
and had been the law in those parts
for years, evading transfer and passing
up promotion with the single-minded
assurance of one who has found his
métier for life. In Middlehope law had
to adapt itself to special conditions, and
walk hand in hand with custom, which
provided the main system by which
behaviour was regulated. One assault
from an intruder, and the whole valley
would clam up and present a united
front of impenetrable ignorance, solid as a
Roman shield-wall, in defence of its own
people and its immemorial sanctity.

Moon was a large, calm, quiet man
with a poker face, and hands as broad
as spades and could look phlegmatic,
and even stupid, at will, but was neither.
And there was nobody better qualified
to dissect the situation in Middlehope,

41

a month or so after Rainbow's house-warming. He and George had both been in court during the morning, and were snatching a quick lunch together in Comerbourne before returning to the rest of the work-load, which at the beginning of October was relatively light.

"Well, how are things in your barony?" asked George. "And how did the harvest supper go off?"

"You're informed that far, are you?" said Moon thoughtfully. "What would you expect? The vicar'd accepted the offer of the chap's house, folks couldn't stay away without making the vicar miserable, so the turnout was much the same as usual. Down a bit, though, and the Rev. couldn't help noticing, and anyhow, by then I doubt if he was much surprised. He does fall over himself to think the best of everybody, but he can learn. Too late, of course. The man's got a strangle-hold on the choir now, it won't be easy to get it off him again. The professor's taken it philosophically, but it's a blow, all the same. And the grounds are offered again for the hospital fête, and if you ask me they're already arranging all the show pieces for sale, sending out invitations to customers all over the Midlands."

"To be fair," George pointed out, "the hospital may benefit by boosted takings, too."

"It *may*! He *will*! He hasn't ploughed all that money into the place without expecting a handsome profit. He's talking of opening the gardens to the public for charity next summer. There'll be an invisible price-tag on most of those lead sirens of his, and quite a turnover in garden stoneware."

"Oh, so he's talking in terms of next year now. Digging in, Jack! What's the valley going to do about it? They usually manage to weed out the unwanted pretty effectively."

"Trouble is we've left it late, not wanting to throw out any man until we were sure. And then, the vicar being newish and not thoroughly clued up yet made his mistake, and now he's stuck with it, and so are we."

"And what's he really like as organist?" asked George curiously. "From all I hear, he can play any keyboard instrument like nobody's business. Obviously the

Reverend thought he was getting a prize. Does that work out?"

"George, if we've got a resistance movement in the general population, believe me, we've got seething revolution in the choir. You won't hear a voluntary in our church now earlier than Duruflé or Messiaen, or an anthem or a chant or a hymn-tune more than twenty years old. The things he's asking those boys to sing you wouldn't wish on a dog-pack! You should see young Bossie's face, soaring to that high F of his and looking like it tastes vile. All new and fashionable and with-it, I'm sure, but with what? Not harmony, nor melody, that's for certain. And what about all the rest of us, brought up on Welsh hwyl and classical form? Nothing to get our teeth in at all! Congregations are dropping off. You know how frustrating it can be, coming all primed to sing your heart out, and very creditably, mind you, we know what's what; and then to be baulked by a parcel of discords fighting out a life-or-death struggle! No, let him be as expert as he likes, he knows nothing and feels nothing about music. If he did, he'd know what he's stirring up, and believe me, he hasn't got a clue."

George thought of Miss de la Pole, with her finger on the valley's pulse like a family doctor, saying almost absently: "What a pity he isn't in the least degree musical!"

"You do seem to have acquired a king-sized headache," he said with sympathy. "You've frozen out tougher propositions before, though. What's so special about this one?"

"A hide like a rhinoceros," said Sergeant Moon succinctly, "and far better insulation. With the money he's got he can isolate himself inside his own world, apart from actual functions at which he has to appear officially. He can bring in his own society, be independent of us and anything we may feel about him. Do you realise we've never had a rich man living among us since the eighteenth century? The mistake was ever to let him in. Now he's in I'm damned if we know how to get at him."

"Somebody'll find a way," said George, rather too lightly.

"That's what I'm afraid of," agreed

Sergeant Moon, not lightly at all.

"As bad as that? Look, Middlehope has digested some pretty odd customers in its time, and turned them into part of the soil. Is Rainbow really impossible?"

"Others," said Moon seriously, "have blundered in and fought it out with us on equal terms, we can appreciate that. They end up talking loftily about the next arrivals as incomers, and then go on to assimilate them. Nobody's going to assimilate Rainbow, he isn't fighting it out on equal or any terms. He came in and asserted his own terms, no question of adapting, no question of parleying or feeling his way, no acknowledgement that Middlehope has any identity of its own. Have you ever walked round with a twig of blackthorn stuck in your sock? He's got to go! He's something we can't afford. He cripples us. So something's got to be done. The hell of it is, everybody's asking, what?"

And well they might, where the foreign body was fully provided with funds, society, interests of his own, independent of the community in which he had set up house. Even if they gradually froze him out of all the offices he had acquired — and that would take some doing! — he still had space and wealth enough, transport to where he was welcome, the means to import his own kind to fill any gaps left by the defection of the natives. He was the least vulnerable intruder with whom Middlehope had ever had to deal. What had begun almost as a joke began to look like a serious problem. You cannot drop a large foreign object into a still and mantled pool without starting dangerous and disruptive ripples.

"What about his wife?" George wondered. "How're they making out with her? She could well be the last straw."

"Ah!" said Sergeant Moon cryptically, and sat thinking for half a minute before he expressed any further opinion. "Now there we're up against a different problem. How did he ever come by her, in the first place? And if you know what to make of her, you tell me, because *we* don't! All that Estee Lauder and haute couture, and sports car and all, and she breezes into the shop and asks for Woodbines, and cheerfully, too. Or drops off when Charlie's frying, just by the way when she smells the oil, and picks up a paper-full of fish and chips. Not when he's with her, but then, he seldom is. And still looking like a million dollars, with all the aplomb in the world. I bet she does the lady of the manor as to the manor born — if you'll pass over the pun. Out of the manor she looks the same but acts different. As if she'd bust out of school. And I tell you this, she fetches a few of her husband's mates buzzing like bees round a flower — that big fair fellow who's been advising on marketing some of the Mottisham Abbey stuff, for one — but there's more than one local chap been risking his fingers round the fire, too. And I wouldn't say but what she enjoys them just as much, if not more. Novelty, I reckon. Most people thought she'd be bored to hell, stuck up there in the hills at the back of beyond, but if you ask me, she's not losing any sleep over being rusticated, the other way round, in fact. It's been an eye-opener."

"I suppose he hasn't got her into the Women's Institute yet?" said George, and had to smile at the idea.

"No, he does the joining, she presides at home and looks handsome. And keeps his friends and rivals coming," said Moon with shrewd perception, "so he knows what they're up to. But as far as public functions go, her job is just to be his consort. I don't think public distinction for her was ever in the contract."

★ ★ ★

At St Eata's church in Abbot's Bale it was the custom of the trebles, during the sermon, to amuse themselves with various ingenious games invented by themselves. The choir-stalls, part of the elaborate renovations perpetrated in the nineteenth century, were deep, and covered a multitude of sins. The boys on the *decani* side had to be wary, since a couple of the tenors behind them were tall enough to see down into the stall in front, even when seated, but happily they were also the two who were most likely to be dozing themselves. The Reverend Stephen's sermons were painstaking and worthy, but not exciting. They also tended to end abruptly, which gave an added spice of danger to some of the games. Passing the chocolate orange, for instance (orange by courtesy of Toffee Bill, whose mother kept the village shop, and paid for by communal funds!), entailed slipping the orange from hand to hand all along the *cantoris* side to the altar end of the stalls, each boy detaching one section for himself, whereupon Ginger Gibbs, last in the line, had the hair-raising job of lobbing the remnant, precariously rewrapped in its gold foil, across the intervening space to Bossie Jarvis on the *decani* side, so that the progress could continue along that stall, too. Nobody had yet thought of a way of getting the few remaining sections across the other end, in full view of the congregation. If any survived, the direction had to be reversed. Judging the right instant to throw required immense coolness and precision. Neither Ginger nor Bossie had ever yet been caught in the act.

There were other pursuits, of course. Those who still carried clean handkerchiefs sometimes tied them into animal shapes, and gave puppet-shows, mainly for their own stall, but sometimes, snatching the right moment, above the desktop for the line opposite. Consequences also had its days, with appropriate variations. Sometimes Bossie, at one end, started a paper slip with the invented name of the dear departed, and each boy after him added one line of the epitaph to appear on his tombstone. But on this particular Sunday it was a similar game played with lines extracted from hymns. This was too difficult to be taken beyond the quatrain, and the fourth participant, if stuck, was allowed to invent his line without being tied to actual hymns. The system had just produced the following:

'The voice says, Cry. What shall we cry?
When heated in the chase,
Behold, the bridegroom draweth nigh
With his arm round amazing Grace.'

Resulting giggles had to be suppressed, and the next player could start a new stanza, in this case generously enough with a simple line:

'This is the first of days',

to which Spuggy Price, always enterprising, added:

'When our heads are bowed with woe',

and Toffee Bill contributed:

'Let our choir new anthems raise'.

The manuscript had now reached Bossie, just as the vicar concluded his sermon, as suddenly as ever, and announced the next hymn. Number 193, 'Jesu, Lover of my soul'. Now this, thought Bossie contentedly, as the congregation squared up hopefully for 'Aberystwyth', is one he can't spoil. Even if he chose 'Hollingside', instead, that would be only a shade less satisfying than the majestic Welsh harmonies. Only the rest of the choir rose apathetically. Bossie, for once, had missed practice, owing to the slight aftermath of a visit to the dentist, and the sound of a completely strange, complicated and extremely uncongenial tune rolling down from the organ-loft caused his jaw to drop, and his eyes to pop out like hat-pegs with indignation. He could even spoil this! Here on the edge of Wales, in a parish of fervent singers, who but Rainbow would have dared to ditch something as splendid as 'Aberystwyth' for this trendy drivel?

Bossie grasped the pencil and wrote the final line of the quatrain so violently that he pushed holes in the paper:

'Rainbow's got to go!' Underlined savagely, and with the added note below: 'In the furnace-room after service. Council of war!'

★ ★ ★

They sat on upturned boxes among the coke, and there wasn't a dissentient voice among them.

"Our choir's been made to raise new anthems long enough," said Bossie grimly, setting his rounded but resolute jaw. "The others are just as fed-up as we are, and dislike him just as much, and if he stays here much longer somebody's going to get desperate and dot him one, or set his house on fire, or something. Because he's never going to fit in, he's all wrong, and he's *got to go!*"

"You're only saying what everybody's been saying for weeks now," Ginger reminded him reasonably. He was a solid, sensible boy, large for his thirteen years, freckled and sandy, but placid of disposition instead of fiery. "They shut up if they think we're listening, but you should have heard the basses letting fly the other night, after he produced this new tune. They didn't know I was still there. But if they can't think of any way of getting rid of him, what do you reckon we can do?"

"He won't go easily," said Toffee Bill gloomily. His mother's shop had not benefited at all from the coming of the Rainbows, who had most of their exotic goods delivered from Comerbourne. Middlehope was good enough to exploit and patronise, but not to mix with; except, of course, its top layers, where layers had never played much part before. The pub didn't benefit, either, drinks were sent up by the crate from dealers in Birmingham. "He's got that house all poshed up, he won't let go of it now, after all the money he's spent, not unless he's druv out. And I don't know how you set about that."

"Grown-ups are too squeamish," said Bossie darkly. "What's the use of fair means, if they don't work? They've been trying to chill him out for ages, ever since they found out what he's like, but he doesn't even notice. As long as he's running everything in sight his way, he doesn't care whether people like him or not."

"Well, that's what I'm saying. If he doesn't care, freezing him out isn't going to work, is it?" Toffee Bill, treasurer of the gang's funds and adviser on best-buys in the sweet world, expert on special offers, competitions and bonus bars, was the thinnest child in the choir, being blessed with one of those metabolisms that can deal with huge amounts of food without putting on an ounce of flesh. His voice was passable, but nothing to write home about, but his value to the group was immense, and they would have resigned *en masse* if his tenure had been threatened. He was, however, a pessimist, necessary ballast to any company that included Spuggy Price, the fiercest and most daring of ten-year-olds, and owner of a light, floating voice, good for at least three years yet, and understudy to Bossie's mellifluous solo act.

"We could scare him off with a ghost," this diminutive genius offered brightly. Three suppressive voices at once opined that of all people, Rainbow would be the last to believe in ghosts, since he didn't believe in anything he couldn't buy, sell or boss. "Besides, he's been in the house more than four months now, where's this ghost been all that time? He'd laugh his head off!"

"He wouldn't if everybody else was laughing," said Bossie thoughtfully. "Laughing at *him*! That's the one thing he wouldn't be able to stand. He can't be all that sure of his ground, he's always been a townie until now, this is a new venture for him. We've let it go on too long, but it's still new. Once shake him, and he won't think it worthwhile fighting it out, he'll make off to the town again. But it's got to be a real shocker to prise him loose. After all, he can sell the house, can't he? It's all done up beautifully, he needn't lose on it, it's a walk-in job, ready for occupation. He'd realise and get out. *If* we can make him a laughing-stock."

He had them all eating out of his hand by this time, as he usually could do at need, if only by reason of his overwhelming vocabulary. Bossie was twelve years old, only child of a marriage between a classically-educated intellectual and a shrewd, practical farmer's daughter, brains on both sides of his parentage, and an insatiable thirst for knowledge in the product. He was relatively small for his age, but compact and tough, as plain as the plainest pike-staff that ever carried a deadly pike, with corrective glasses to eradicate the infant consequences of what is technically termed a lazy eye. His colouring was nondescript brown, with thick dun-coloured hair that grew in all directions, and unnerving hazel eyes enlarged unequally behind their therapeutic lenses, which in a few years he would discard, to become disarmingly human. Altogether, a walking time-bomb, propelled by precocious intuitions and abilities, and restrained by a classical and liberal education. He knew he was formidable, but he didn't know how formidable.

"And how do we do that?" wondered Ginger, reserving judgement.

"Well, he's a dealer in antiques, isn't he? That's how he's made his money, and that's his weakness, because you can't know everything about everything, and antiques is practically everything. So if we hooked him on an antique that would get him foaming at the mouth, thinking he'd cornered a fortune, and then show him up either as a cheat who was pinching something belonging to someone else, or a fool who's fallen for a common forgery — you think he'd stand up to that? I don't! He's got a reputation to lose in the trade. He'd spread his wings and fly, as fast and quietly as he could, and hope nobody outside here would ever hear of it."

They mulled that over in silence for some moments, and found but one fault in it. Ginger dispiritedly put it into words. "That sounds all very well. But we haven't got an antique to shove under his nose, real or fake. And even if we had, we wouldn't know how to set about it."

"But *I* have," said Bossie portentously, sinking his voice to hollow depths of conspiracy. "And *I DO!*"

★ ★ ★

"Dad," demanded Bossie, emerging with knitted brows from behind an enormous book containing full-page illustrations from the Stonyhurst Gospels, "how late did they go on writing in uncials?"

Sam barely looked up from his desk, and showed no excitement or curiosity whatever at this sudden enquiry. No question from Bossie, on any subject from Egyptian hieroglyphs to nuclear physics, could surprise his parents. He was an insatiable sponge for knowledge of all kinds.

"Oh, it petered out round about the eighth to the ninth century, I suppose."

"Pity!" said Bossie. "It's easy to read. How did they write after that, then?"

"It got more and more loose and cursive, and a lot harder to read, you're right there."

"Where can I find a copy, say about

late thirteenth century?"

Sam got up good-naturedly, and reached down a book almost as large, and opened it for him at one of the facsimile plates. "There you are, probably rather a better script than most, it's out of a Benedictine chartulary, thirteenth century. They were letting out some land at farm. That's a fair sample." He went back to his work without further question.

Bossie studied the page before him critically, and jutted a thoughtful lip. "What's this word here? Look! 'p'tin' suis, et terra Fereholt cu' p'tin' suis'. 'P'tin' isn't a proper word." His Latin was good, but he had not so far been called upon to cope with unextended mediaeval examples.

"Those are the contractions the clerks made," Sam reassured him absently. "With all the copying they had to do, they adopted a method of shorthand. They could understand and translate it, even if their bosses couldn't. And probably a lot of their bosses couldn't read, anyway, so they had to leave it to the clerks. 'P'tin' suis' is 'its appurtenances'. They were farming out

60

some piece of land you didn't name 'with its appurtenances, and the land of Fereholt with *its* appurtenances'."

"Not a bad idea, shortening everything like that," Bossie approved, with a purposeful gleam in his eye, as though he had seen a short cut round a laborious chore. "Can I borrow this for tonight?"

"Sure! Bring it back when you've done. Want the Latin dictionary? Or shall I extend the whole page for you, so you can read it yourself?" And he pushed back his chair, and was really looking at his son now, willing to ditch his own current labours to assist in whatever Bossie was grappling with.

"No, thanks, that's all right." Bossie sensed that his disclaimer had been a shade hasty, which might indicate an undertaking on the suspect side. But he knew all the words calculated to intimidate parents, and was adroit in using them. "It's all right for me to *ask*," he explained generously, "but I mustn't let you help me." And drawing breath for the *coup de grâce*, "It's for a SPECIAL PROJECT!" he said with enormous dignity, and bore the chartulary of the Benedictine brothers away to his own room.

★ ★ ★

During the week following these curious activities of Bossie Jarvis, Arthur Everard Rainbow came home from choir practice somewhat later than usual, and instead of dropping his music-case casually on the hall table, carried it through to his own sacred study; clasped under his arm with jealous fondness. His wife, who had sailed out from her drawing-room to meet him, letting out with her floating skirts the murmur of voices and the sound of well-produced string music, noted his passage with mild interest, went back to her friends with a shrug and a private smile, and said, without any particular intent, and without paying much attention to the words she used:

"Arthur'll be in in a few moments. He must have discovered an unknown Bach score. I should think, he's hugging his music-case with a lover's gleam in his eye. You never know where you'll strike gold in our business, do you? Even at choir practice it can happen."

There were at least a dozen people in the room at the time. He liked her to stage her musical evenings when he was due to be missing for most of the time, it gave a relaxed atmosphere in which tongues might be loosened and defences lowered. That way she gathered more information, as they dropped their guard. Drinks had little effect upon her, he was pretty sure her guests never got much in return for their own advances.

She knew, in any case, that they were always on the alert.

"Turn up the volume, Colin," she mimed across the room. "Just a little!" And she sat down again in her old place, diplomatically between Charles Goddard and John Stubbs, neither of whom had a directly profitable interest in antiques, whatever their private passions, and closed her eyes to listen seriously to Schubert. She never even noticed when her husband came in, discreet, hushing comment with a finger on his lips because of the music, and on those lips, half-concealed, a rapt, anticipatory smile that had nothing whatever to do with

Schubert, and exulted in the ignorance of his guests and colleagues.

It was precisely eight days after this that the Reverend Stephen Baines received a telephone call at the early hour of seven in the morning.

"This is Barbara Rainbow, vicar. I'm sorry to worry you at this hour, but . . . " She sounded curiously hesitant, dubious of her own wisdom in telephoning at all. "I'm probably troubling you over nothing, but I do wonder — did my husband, by any chance, say anything last night about going on somewhere else after practice? Something could have come up suddenly, he has been known to run off somewhere on business without remembering to let me know." Her voice was picking its way with distaste, reluctant to expose the more arid places of the Rainbow marriage. But not a doubt of it, she was seriously worried. "He didn't come home," she said flatly. "That could happen, and of course he's perfectly capable of looking after himself. But I've still had no word, and I did rather expect him to 'phone before now. I won't say I'm alarmed, there's probably no cause to be. But

I just wondered if he'd mentioned any further plans when practice ended." And she added, as though she had already taken thought to cover all eventualities: "His car is here, you see. He walked to church, he usually does."

"I see," said the Reverend Stephen rather blankly. "No, all he did say was that he was staying to try over some new music he'd brought, so he would lock up for the night. Nothing about going on anywhere else afterwards. I wonder — you didn't try contacting anyone last night?" He was not sure himself whether he meant the police or some of Rainbow's business associates.

"No. I'm used to occasional abrupt departures, after all. He works on an opportunist basis at times. And one doesn't start an alarm in the middle of the night without feeling sure it's necessary, and I didn't — I don't feel sure of that at all. But now . . . You left him alone there at the church, then?"

"Yes, at about half past eight, the usual time. I heard him playing when I left, I think all the choir had already gone home. Would you like me to . . . ? Do you think we should notify . . . ?"

"No. don't worry," said Barbara. "I expect it's perfectly all right. I'll call the shops, and see if he's been in touch there." Rainbow had two shops, one in Birmingham, one in Worcester, where carefully selected manageresses looked after his interests. "He's probably gone haring off after treasure trove somewhere." He might, for instance, have felt an urge to resort to the society of the Birmingham manageress, who was an efficient and accommodating blonde, appreciated as a mistress of long standing, but not socially equipped to figure as his wife. But that Barbara refrained from saying. "Thanks, anyway! Don't worry about it!"

But the Reverend Stephen, once he had hung up, immediately began to worry, all the same, and there was nothing to be done but go and look for himself in the church and the organ-loft, to see if by any chance Rainbow had left his music there, or some other sign of his presence. Even healthy-looking men in their prime have been known to succumb to heart attacks without warning. He didn't really expect anything of that kind. He was not, in fact, expecting to find, as he did, the church door unlocked, Rainbow's music-case lying unfastened on the organ-bench, and a new voluntary still in place on the stand. That jolted him slightly. It was out of character for Rainbow to leave any of his possessions lying about. But there was no sign of the man himself anywhere in the church.

The vicar hardly knew why he found it necessary to walk all round the paths of his churchyard, since there was no reason whatever why even a Rainbow suddenly overtaken by illness should be lying helpless among the graves, when his music was still withindoors. But the Reverend Stephen was a thorough man, and circled his church conscientiously by the grassy path that threaded its way close to the walls. Under the tower the oldest gravestones clustered like massive, broken teeth, upright headstones leaning out of true, solid table-tombs grown over with moss in their lettering, and deep in long grass bleaching to autumn, because in such a huddle it was almost impossible to mow or even to scythe.

The vicar turned the corner of the tower, and clucked mild annoyance, because somebody had thrown down what looked like some old, dark rags among the long grass, or else the wind had blown them there, or some playful pup dragged them in. Dogs were not frowned upon in St Eata's churchyard. The Reverend Stephen looked upon them as among the most innocent and confiding, if rowdy, of God's creatures.

He went aside from the path to remove the offence, and froze after two paces. The dark rags had gained a distinct shape, had matter within them, had sprayed the table-tomb and surrounding stones with a sparse, blackened rain. The shape was grotesque, as if someone had loosed a heavy press at speed upon a human form, and squashed it into fragments, as some nut-crackers reduce a walnut to splintered pulp. But there was still a discernible, even a recognisable, head. There was a face, upturned, open-mouthed, open-eyed. The fall that had shattered all other bones had left this identifying countenance unmarked, the back of the skull lolling in the thick verdure beneath it.

Rainbow had had every reason for absenting himself from his somewhat equivocal connubial couch. He stared at the October sky past the Reverend Stephen's head, and seemed almost immune to the ruin of his body. There was even a look of desperate eagerness left glaring from his fixed features, as though he had died with his eye upon the crock of gold.

3

THE Reverend Stephen was a conscientious soul who knew all about the citizen's duty where murder or mayhem were in question, or even the self-violence that could hardly he associated with Rainbow. He drew back from the appalling wreckage among the graves with great care, marking his path in case some other, less innocent, had also trodden here during the night, and went to call the police, whose job this clearly was. But he was so far adopted into the tribal structure of Middlehope that it never occurred to him to call anyone but Sergeant Moon.

Homicide might live in Comerbourne. Here in Middlehope Sergeant Moon was the official guardian of the tribe's peace, to be trusted absolutely, and turned to in all emergencies. The Reverend Stephen never for one moment entertained the idea of notifying Barbara Rainbow of her husband's present whereabouts and present state. Nor did it occur to him that he was treating her as a woman of the tribe, not an alien from the outer world. Middlehope had spread a wing over her from that moment, whether she knew it or not.

"Oh, yes, quite dead," said the vicar simply, at ease with the man to whom he spoke. "He's broken to pieces, you see. He must have come off the tower, he couldn't have been shattered like that any other way. Yes, it was his wife who rang me, fretting about him not coming home. I think he sometimes didn't, but this time she hadn't any clues, and she was troubled." A good Biblical word, troubled. "I haven't told anyone, and nobody's likely to go through there, not close, I thought better let well alone rather than mount a guard. No, I haven't said a word to her."

"All right, sir," said Sergeant Moon briskly, "you go and just keep a discreet eye on the place, and fend people off it if need be, and I'll be with you in ten minutes."

"She mustn't see him, you know," said the vicar, and blushed to hear himself giving advice to an old hand like the sergeant. But after all, he had seen what was left of Rainbow, and as yet Sergeant Moon hadn't. "I suppose it's properly my job to tell the widow . . . ?"

"We'll take care of all that," said Moon imperturbably, and cleared the line in order to get through direct to head-quarters at Comerbourne.

"Oh, *no!*" protested George, confronted with this altogether too apt confirmation of the sergeant's forebodings. "You'll have to give up prophecy, Jack, you're too unnerving."

"Could be accident," said Moon, without much confidence. "Sounds as if he fell from the church tower. I'm on my way, and I've called the doc."

"Right, we'll be with you in twenty minutes."

In the event it took the squad a full half-hour to reach Abbot's Bale, since the morning rush was in full swing, and the roads congested. But within an hour the whole grisly apparatus connected with sudden and suspect death had arrived, and was grouped about all that remained of Arthur Everard Rainbow.

The police doctor, confronted with this wreckage, shrugged his helplessness, testified unnecessarily to the fact that life was extinct, opined that it had been extinct for many hours, almost certainly all night, and left it to the pathologist to go into detail, since this was now obviously his affair. The photographer shot a great deal of film, and the forensic scientist, arriving last, looked down at the body, looked up at the tower, looming close over the spot, and wondered whether he was needed at all.

"Not much doubt where he fell from, is there?" he observed mildly. "Pretty plain case of accident, wouldn't you say?" He had not, so far, taken a close look at the set-up.

"On the face of it, yes," agreed George, "except that I don't much like its face. There are grazes on his palms, and the balls of his fingers, for one thing, white marks of what looks like stone-dust, and the same under his finger-nails, as well as what I think you may find to be fragments of moss. And since he can hardly have done any scrabbling about on the stones here after he hit, if I'm right the debris is from up there."

"He'd try to grab hold and save himself if he found himself falling," suggested the devil's advocate, already interested.

"Why should he find himself falling? There doesn't seem to be a large chunk of masonry that's come down with him, or anything like that. And though I haven't been up there, I wouldn't mind betting that parapet is breast-high. You don't overbalance over a barrier like that. Not to mention the question of what he was doing up on top in the first place."

"Hmmm, that's true. They'd hardly keep the organ out on the leads, would they? Well, now, let's have a look, before the doc takes him away." And delicately he began to move round the rim of the scene, looking at grass-blades and the scarred mosses on the stones. Dr Reece Goodwin, a round, bouncing, energetic ball of a man, well into his sixties but looking fifteen years younger, was kneeling beside the body, touching and probing with spatulate fingers.

"An odd chance, he fell with all the lower part of him on this table tomb and these two headstones, smashed himself to pieces from the waist down, but he came down head and shoulders in this thick tangle of grass and brambles. Nothing but superficial damage, scratches and impact grazes to the head. And yet he's bled from the back of the skull, and I think we're going to find there's an indented wound here — resting against nothing but all this cushiony vegetation. And he certainly never moved after he hit."

"Interesting" said George. "It looks as if you've got yourself a job this afternoon."

Dr Goodwin bounded up from his knees, and scrubbed his hands vigorously. "So it seems! Right now I wouldn't give you a precise cause of death, obvious though it may seem. Can I have him now?"

So that was that. A post-mortem was essential, and the shadow of murder was already looming as the shadow of the tower crept round to mark the passing of noon. A man falling by accident may certainly claw at the stones to try to arrest his fall. Even a suicide may change his mind at the last moment, and try to cling to the world he has set out to abandon. But in neither case is he likely to end up with his head the most intact part of him after the fall, cushioned in vegetation, and yet with an indented wound at the back of his skull.

They hoisted the rag-doll remains of Rainbow into a plastic sheet, packed him into a shell, and stowed him away in Reece Goodwin's van for his journey to the hospital mortuary in Comerbourne. The vicar, hovering unhappily in the background, was almost relieved when he was asked if the police might borrow the parish hall as an incident room, and was left there with Sergeant Moon to make a formal statement, while Detective Sergeant Brice and Constables Reynolds and Collins began a methodical examination of the church from nave to tower, layer by layer, and George, ruefully shouldering the most distasteful duty left, went in person to break the news to Barbara Rainbow.

He was halfway up the drive, among the calculated spaces and tastefully positioned statuary, when it dawned on him that while the widow might be badly shaken by this death, possibly no one in the world would be really sorry. In his own business circles Rainbow appeared to have been watched, respected, envied and copied, but never actually liked. In this valley he had made himself not so much detested as dangerous, and not to be tolerated, like a disease, Middlehope would breathe more freely now that he was gone. And the spectacular Barbara?

She opened the door to him herself, in grey slacks and a silk shirt, her hair down round her shoulders; and her black brows, drawn together over eyes focused somewhere far beyond him, suddenly smoothed out in relief. She recognised him gladly. Recalling the party intimacy, she said: "George . . . !" and even launched upon a genuine, if anxious, smile, and then she looked more closely, and grew cool and still, and certain of a thunderbolt. "No," she said, "I'm sorry! That was presumptuous. It's Superintendent Felse isn't it? This is official."

"I'm afraid so," said George.

"Come in! As a matter of fact," she said, closing the door upon the world and leading the way into the small drawing-room where Rainbow's grand piano stood, "I've just called the police down the valley. Do sit down! But you . . . you're C.I.D, aren't you? How could you be involved?" The dark eyes were intent and guarded, and she was pale. Hardly any make-up, he realised, and as beautiful as ever. "I've been calling his shops, and his dealers, and everybody I could think of who might know his movements, ever since I called the vicar, early this morning. Nobody knows anything. So finally I called the police. But just the police. That wouldn't come straight to you. You must have come into it some other way. And you do know something, don't you?"

"The vicar called Sergeant Moon," said George, "who called me. For sufficient reason."

"Yours is the criminal division," she said deliberately. "Are you suggesting there's something criminal involved?"

It was an eventuality which had never occurred to him, though all too clearly it had to her. He could not believe that she was acting or prevaricating. The first thing that had occurred to her, when her husband vanished without trace, was that he had excellent reason for doing so. What she dreaded was something that would involve her loyalty. Not her integrity. Not her affection. George was suddenly sure that the news he was actually bringing would be very much easier to bear.

"Not as you mean. No question of any criminal act on your husband's part. After your morning call the vicar was naturally worried, and went to see if there was any suggestion to be found in the church. He found a situation which made him call our department at once. Your husband is dead, Mrs Rainbow. It looks as if he fell to his death from the church tower last night. I'm sorry to be the bearer of such news."

He'd been right to go ahead bluntly with the fact. And the first thing he saw in her, or was almost certain he saw, was that she had never for a moment considered this possibility. Either that, or she was an actress right out of his experience. Her eyes flared wide open, her face blanched with shock, her hands, which had been bunched into doubled fists a moment before, lay loose in her lap. The second thing he saw, as she stirred slowly out of her stillness, was that she had glimpsed a marvellous light at the end of a long and still suspect tunnel. *So that was all!* He was dead, and she hadn't killed him, or even willed his death. Simply, he wasn't there any more!

"Are you sure?" she said in a muted, wary voice, letting the syllables slide out one by one as if they had to carry passports. "Arthur's dead? But how could it happen? Why should he fall from the tower? Why should he even climb the tower? All he wanted was the organ, and the choir to go with it." The single virtue Rainbow had possessed hit her suddenly, she knotted her hands again, and rocked like a genuine widow. "He did care for music, you know! Only he never really felt it in his bones."

His bones were in splinters from the waist down, and he was almost excessively dead. George experienced her brief, guilty, unloving pity, and understood it. She didn't really owe very much.

"You'll want to ask me questions." she said reasonably. "Where is he? Do you need me to — to identify him, or anything?"

"That won't be necessary," said George. "But you'll understand that his death presents something of a problem, and we shall have to collect all the information possible that can shed any light on it. For instance, it seems hardly likely that he set out to take his own life."

"No, he never would," said Barbara positively.

"The idea of an accidental fall presents difficulties, too."

"I understand," she said bluntly. "You can't rule out the possibility that someone else had a hand in it. It's all right, I know where I stand now. The marriage partner is normally the first suspect. You'll want access to all his papers and accounts. You'd better have the key of his office now, everything in it is just as he left it. And you'll want a statement from me, about his movements yesterday, and mine."

"I'll send someone later to get a formal statement. Now just tell me. Things were

81

as usual yesterday? He went to choir practice at the usual time? There was nothing out of the way in his manner?"

"Everything was just the same as ever. He always walked to the church, it's not far by the side gate. He went out at the usual time, and he told me he'd be late back, because he wanted to get in some practice after the choir left. That's why I wasn't worried until around midnight. He could easily have stopped in at the vicar's afterwards, and sat talking about his plans for the season's music. He intended some drastic changes. They weren't too popular with the choir. Some modern music is very ungrateful stuff for voices. I was here alone all the evening, and went to bed without waiting for him. Even when I woke up later, and found he still hadn't come in, I can't say I was really worried. He didn't invariably consult me, or even warn me, before taking off on business at a moment's notice. And besides, nobody could have started much of a hunt for him in the middle of the night. But when there was no telephone call this morning, and his car was still in the garage. I thought

I'd better make some discreet enquiries. That was when I called the vicar, and since then I've called everyone I could think of, half a dozen dealers, both the shops, even Charles Goddard in Comerbourne, and John Stubbs down at Mottisham. And then you came. And that's all. Oh, and I'll give you his solicitor's name and number. As far as I know, they hold his will."

She was perfectly in command of herself and her situation now, and her composure in speaking of such details as her husband's will was completely detached and impersonal, as though the disposal of his worldly goods had nothing to do with her, and could hardly affect her.

"And what happens about the funeral arrangements? I suppose there has to be an inquest. And then will they release his body? I suppose I ought to call in a firm to take responsibility, in any case."

"It would be wise," George agreed. "I'd like the addresses of the shops. And I will take the office key, with your permission. We shall probably have to disturb you occasionally during the next few days, but we'll try not to upset your life more than we have to. You have no servants living in the house?"

"To vouch for my movements last night?" she said with a faint, grim smile. "No, I'm afraid you'll have to take, or doubt, my word for it. There are two girls who come in, mornings, and help out if I have a dinner-party. And a woman who comes in twice a week to clean. All from the village. I'll give you their names, too."

Nothing could have been more open or more practical. She handed him the freedom of the house and of all her husband's papers and records, as though they were now nothing to do with her. As though, in fact, she felt the whole load of this house, this business, this association, lifted from her, and was undertaking the final chore of handing over to someone else with the greatest equanimity. The end of an employment. Rather an abrupt end, but the times were such that sudden redundancies were commonplace.

It occurred to him as he was leaving that there was even a note of curious anticipation in her practicality, rather as though the redundancy did not come amiss to her, almost as though she already had some other and more congenial situation in mind. It sent him away wondering how accurate his judgement of her had been, and how good an actress she could be at need. For there was no blinking the fact that Rainbow had not projected the image of a successful marriage so much as that of an efficient working partnership, and the lady had a field of admirers as long as Middlehope itself, besides the outsiders from Rainbow's world. Now just how do all these hopeful swains stand, George wondered, now she's a widow?

* * *

Sergeant Moon and Detective-Constable Barnes, who was a Middlehope man himself, were making the rounds of the nearest houses to the church, in search of someone, somewhere, who would admit to having seen, or heard, or even thought, anything during the past twenty-four hours. They were both guileful and resourceful men, well versed in the ways of their neighbours, and they made every approach obliquely, with mild deception in every phrase. But neither of them was surprised to find that the news had flown before them, even though no curious onlookers had had to be chased away from the churchyard. However deviously they circled the real reason for their enquiries, just as deviously the interrogated counter-circled, well aware of what had happened to Rainbow, and impervious in the armour of ignorance. Nobody saw anything, nobody heard anything, nobody knew anything.

"Which could well be true," admitted Barnes, comparing notes after an hour's activity. "Because I reckon this was timed well on, round about ten if not after, and it would be dark, and there aren't any houses so near that one heavy, dull fall, with no after-sounds, would get people rushing out to see what had happened. But no bones about it, the result would be the same if nine or ten of us had seen him shoved over the parapet." It was the measure of his entrenched loyalties that even in a police matter he said 'us' and not 'them', a fact which Sergeant Moon perfectly understood.

As for the choir, there was no way of getting at the boys until they were home from school and under the guardianship of their parents, and the men, scattered at work between upland farms, small craft workshops, and the factories of Comerbourne, had better also be left until evening. When, of course, they would say they went straight home after practice, and knew nothing further about anything connected with Rainbow. Still, they had to be asked.

In the post-mortem room at Comerbourne George watched what he had grown used to after many experiences, but would much rather not have had to watch. Mortality was an abstract idea, having its own solemn dignity, if not beauty, but even mortality disintegrated under the hands of Reece Goodwin, and there, but for the grace of God, went every one of us, identity and all, into sample-jars and dog-meat. The fact that the remains would undoubtedly be reassembled as decently as possible, and far beyond what would have been thought possible, hardly mitigated the harshness of this dissection.

And yet it was meant for the protection of those still living, and the provision of justice towards this one, dead, and he had learned to accept it. To be the pathologist was quite a different discipline. The more impossible the task of extracting information from the material provided, the more enthusiastic did Reece Goodwin become. But this one was fresh and relatively simple, and he had to draw his ardours from its few subtleties.

"Now this," he said didactically, probing round the head of the corpse with delicate, passionate fingers, "presents a very interesting problem. This head wound, you can see, is so situated that it cannot possibly have arisen in the course of impact after his fall. It lies low at the back of the skull, and is long and narrow and deeply indented, and was clearly inflicted before death, though probably very shortly before. It might well have been enough to cause death, if these multiple injuries received in the impact hadn't intervened. If they really did intervene! He was not dead, or even unconscious, when he fell or was hoisted over the coping, for this stuff we've isolated from under his finger-nails, and these markings on his palms, are certainly traces of stone-dust — we'll go into the kind! — and fine mosses. He was still able to claw at safety."

"And he couldn't have made any such motions after his fall?" George asked.

"After his fall he was most definitely dead. Once for all. In fact, what is particularly interesting, though he was alive enough to try and cling to the stone at the top, he may very well have been dead before he hit at the bottom. One rather hopes he was."

"One does," agreed George drily. The thought that Rainbow might have made his exit in the mild autumn night between assault and violation, in mid-air, was curiously calming. Almost like being taken up to heaven in a fiery chariot, or by liberal-minded angels. If heaven was Rainbow's destination? It did seem, to put it moderately, rather excessive. There should have been a sort of commercial limbo.

"These obvious multiple injuries, though they did spatter the neighbouring stones, actually shed very little blood. I can't tell you whether the head wound caused his death, or the impact. My guess would be, he was as good as dead when he landed, but it is a guess. I've got a lot of work to do on him before I can be more precise."

"Then the head wound is the only one that can't have been either self-inflicted, or the result of the fall?" George insisted.

"That's right, it can't, and it's the only one. Somebody hit him from behind, fairly low at the back of the skull. And with fell intent, and a long, narrow and very solid instrument. The marvel is that he was conscious enough to claw at the parapet as he went over, after such a clout. But take if from me, he was. He did."

"Would there have been much bleeding?"

"I doubt if there was time. Seems to me it was a fast bash, and a heave over the edge. But you may find traces where it happened."

"Then there may also be matter useful to us, still in the wound. Any notion yet of what kind? Fragments of rust, wood splinters, stone dust?"

"You'll have to wait for the forensic boys to tell you for certain. Any amount of specimens here for them, as soon as I've certified them all. But I'd say, probably stone. Loose bit of coping up there? Edge of a tile? They did an extensive restoration job on the church last century, you said, there could be all sorts of fragments lying around up there."

"I'm heading back there now," said George. "Any idea about timing? It was a fine, mild night to be lying out, shouldn't be anything freakish about the temperature factor."

"He was dead before midnight, I'm certain. Medically it could even have been as early as eight, but you're going to be able to cut down on that end from evidence. I'd say most probably it happened between nine and ten."

"And the vicar left him, still at the organ, about half past eight. Say a couple of hours for everybody in the valley to account for himself. And either they'll all have alibis," prophesied George, "or else none of them will. They stand or fall together up in Middlehope."

He drove back to Abbot's Bale with the tea-time traffic, to confer with Sergeant Moon at the parish hall before joining Detective-Sergeant Brice at the church. Moon's report was exactly what he had expected.

"I've seen all the boys, they all say they went straight home after practice, some of 'em together part of the way, naturally, where they live close. They'd all heard about him being dead, of course, not a hope of the grape-vine failing, up there, in or out of school. No question of shock or surprise, they already knew. All very quiet, very demure, a bit subdued, with a lot of excitement bubbling inside. They aren't sorry, but they are sobered. None of 'em liked him, but this never entered their heads, whatever else they wished him. The men, Barnes is going the rounds now. But the result will be the same."

"And nobody else has turned up a useful fact? Nobody in the pub heard anything? No regulars who failed to show?"

"Nobody saw anything, nobody heard anything, nobody knows anything. And nobody has to issue orders, or even set the example. They all wanted rid of him, and generally speaking they've all got open minds about the rash soul who took steps about it. The consensus of opinion seems to be that the situation wasn't as desperate as all that, and this action is unjustifiably drastic, but all the same . . . Well, you know yourself, alibis are meaningless in Middlehope. When threatened, they close ranks. For all you know," said Moon generously, "it could be anybody. It could be me!"

"Interesting!" said George. "Was it?"

"Well, no, it wasn't. But then," pointed out the sergeant reasonably, "we'd all say that, wouldn't we?"

"Come on," said George, "let's go and see if the church is any more informative."

St Eata's church — a local dedication which occurred in several of the hill villages — dated back to Saxon times, but nothing much of Saxon workmanship was left above-ground, and even the succeeding Early English had largely been patched, built on to, and defaced in several later ages, even before the ambitious nineteenth-century renovation was undertaken. The fabric had ended up as slightly top-heavy neo-Gothic, with the upper part of its old tower rebuilt and made more lofty, with a new battlemented surround. It still had a respectable congregation, and so had escaped the horrid fate of being declared redundant. Its one unchallenged excellence was its organ, an early masterpiece lovingly rebuilt.

"Any amount of people go in and out here most days." said Detective-Sergeant Brice, looking up from the nave towards the organ pipes, towering above the left-hand side of the chancel. "I thought we should have to spend half our time keeping folks out today, but only the vicar's been near. It's as though the place has been tabu from the time they saw us move in. Not that this part has anything much to tell us. It's different once you get up above, where hardly anyone ever goes. We've marked several details for you."

"The organ first," said George.

Rainbow's music-case was still lying on the organ-bench, unfastened, sheet music fanning out from it. George looked round at the demigod's view of the church from this angle, and up at the correctively awesome vista of pipes. Organs are designed to prostrate the onlooker with humility before their vastness and beauty, and exalt their handlers into daemonic self-glorification. But here everything was neat, placid and undisturbed; here there had certainly been no sudden assault, no life and death struggle. The floor was clean, every surface dustless, everything in order.

"Right, now the tower."

Down to the body of the church again, and along to the west end, to the curtained alcove and the narrow stairway that led to the bellringers' room. This, again, was regularly used and scrupulously cleaned, no dust to trap intruding footprints. The looped ropes of an eight-bell peal dangled motionless, their padded grips striped spirally in red, white and blue cotton, like barbers' poles. A fair amount of light came in from Gothic lancets. In one corner an open-treaded stairway, broad, solid and safe, slanted upwards into a narrow, dark trap above. George climbed, and emerged into a sort of attic limbo below the still invisible bells. A stout, boarded floor, roughly finished, an enclosing scent of old timber, and a sense of being suspended in half-light between two worlds. In the far corner another step-ladder, still with broad treads, pursued its upward way. Here people seldom came, and very few of them. Here there was dust, moderately thick, peacefully still, with the furred neatness of undisturbed places.

"Here it gets more interesting," said Brice. "Look here, on this first stair. More than one set of feet has trodden up the middle, mostly the prints are overlaid and scuffed, but here there's one left foot that stepped well to the side of the tread, and the mark's quite clear. We've followed all the tracks up. This one just doesn't seem to occur again, unless he very carefully trod always in the middle where the dust was already disturbed. It looks as if somebody got this far, and then changed his mind."

"And there are two sets of tracks beyond?" asked George.

"Two detectable. Could be more, but

definitely two. But not this one. Or never distinct beyond this point."

The soft dust, securely settled, had taken an excellent impression. An old shoe, trodden down at the heel, unevenly weighted, and with a distinct crack across the sole. A print that suggested a smallish foot in an over-large shoe, the foot of an older man who liked his comfort, and clung to the old friends that ensured it.

"You've isolated and copied everything above that might be useful? Right, up we go!" But even so George trod carefully, up into the dimly-lit bell-chamber, smelling of clean, dry must, and haunted by monstrous, still bronze shapes in the gloom. A large area of floor here, and only a runged ladder continuing the ascent. There was also a quantity of debris stacked in corners, left behind from the renovations, carved stones so weathered that the carving was almost obliterated, bits of voussoirs half worn away with corrosion but retaining a shape someone hadn't wanted to throw away. All too massive to provide handy weapons, but the suggestion was there. And there were two huge but sadly decayed wooden chests, one with a disjointed lid propped back against the wall, and layer below layer of discoloured papers spread in some disorder within. George crossed to look more closely, for though age and damp had marked the contents in brownish ripples, only some of them were filmed with a layer of dust, and even that only superficial, and some of those half-uncovered below were perfectly clear of dust. The lid had not been thus open long, the contents had been only recently disturbed. He read titles of Victorian magazines, *Ivy Leaves*, *Harmsworth Magazine*, *Musical Bits*, and the modest headings of parish magazines. And some older, *Gentleman's Magazine*, *The Grand*, as far back as the late eighteenth century. The floor beside the chest was trodden more or less clear of dust, dappled with treads so that no clear print was visible.

"Somebody was interested," said George.

"Yes, sir, and not so long ago. Maybe more than one, but one very recently indeed. But I doubt if they found much of anything."

"Not to interest Rainbow, one would imagine. This stuff might be treasure to a social historian, but not to an antiquarian in it for the money. No great value there. Unless, of course, there was some unusual item among the collection. We'll have to go through all this in detail, but on the face of it it isn't his cup of tea. Leave it just as it is. And meantime, we'll ask the vicar if anyone has been up here, legitimately, in the last few months. There could be occasions when need arose."

"Well, above here it's by ladder. The dust's been rubbed off the middle of the rungs, as you'd expect, but not much else to be found. No traces of blood, or anything. I'll lead the way."

The ladders, built into place, proceeded by four short stages, making the circuit of the square tower, and brought them out by a low and narrow wooden door into daylight on the leads. The doorway, pointed Gothic in relatively new stone, was accommodated in the wall of the single corner turret, rising nine feet above the general level of the parapet, which was breast-high to a man of middle height.

And abandoned to weather and moss in the corner by the turret lay the obvious fragments of the old stone voussoirs from the former archway, a few pitted and crumbling strips of moulding, a couple of decorative bosses worn to the fragility of shells.

"Any indication of where he went over? It would be this side, wouldn't it?" After that spiral ascent it took a few seconds to regain a sense of direction, but a glance down over the parapet located the spot where Rainbow's body had fallen. And even without Brice's eager demonstration, there were the faint, pale streaks where nails had clawed ineffectively at the crest of the stonework. The embrasures between the merlons of the embattled wall dropped to waist-level. Not so hard, perhaps, to grip a man round the knees and hoist him over the edge. But still improbable for anyone to overbalance and fall. "Yes, that's clear enough. He grabbed for the solid wall on either side of the embrasure."

"And there are two or three dark spots here that could be blood." Brice showed them, incredibly insignificant to be the only signs of a man's death-blow, but blood, almost unquestionably. A fast bash and a heave over the edge, as Reece Goodwin had said.

George went back to the pile of stone fragments in the corner, and stood looking down at them attentively. Moss had bound them into a coagulated mass, a few small tufts of grass had found enough soil at the edges to survive. The one long strip of stony pallor, devoid of its thin green covering, showed like a scar. Something about ten inches long and no more than two wide, slightly curved, had been removed from there recently. A broken piece of moulding from the doorway arch? Whatever it was, the bare leads showed no sign of it now.

"Supposing you had just used a length of stone to break a man's skull, and tipped him over here into the churchyard," said George thoughtfully, "what would you do with the weapon? To make it disappear most effectively?"

"Easy," said Moan promptly. "I'd throw it off the tower on the other side. Not only because that would separate it as far as possible from the body, in a churchyard which I've got to admit is a right tangle, too thickly populated ever to get mown properly — but on that side the congestion is worst and the disintegration most advanced. That's the oldest part. Looking for a slice of stonework there would be like looking for a needle in a haystack."

"Pity," said George with sympathy, "because that's just what you and your boys are going to be doing as from now."

"That's what I was afraid of," agreed Moon with equanimity. "If there's a hunk of local stone around with traces of blood, and not native to where it's lying, we'll get it for you before the light fails. I know this place better than I've ever bothered to get to know the palm of my hand. Mind if I borrow another piece to send after it? One of these bosses — no mistaking that for the one we shall be looking for, I take it?"

He had a way, both reassuring and unnerving, of being entrenched in certainty where the habits and cosmography of his chosen ground were concerned, and of proving right practically all the time.

George was not in the least surprised when the sergeant came to him in the parish hall, around seven o'clock, bearing on a fold of paper a ten-inch sliver of stone, very gently curved, easily wielded in one hand by any well-grown person, and retaining a murderously sharp edge of moulding on its clean side, protected by having lain face-down in the discard pile. It had also, impaled upon this sharp edge, palpable traces of blood and matter, and a few short hairs.

"Sorry I can't guarantee any guilty prints, George," said Moon, easy and unofficial, since they were alone, "but I doubt if we've got the best field for 'em here. But this is the weapon, all right. We've marked the place where it crashed. I was about a couple of yards too far to the left with that boss, but about the same range. You've got a pretty hefty bloke to look for. It was a good throw, and he'd be in a hurry."

There was a mass of statements to be matched up by then, and he sat down and joined in the work as soon as the murder weapon had been despatched to the forensic laboratory. They worked together with maximum placidity and understanding; but the statements were as void as they had both expected.

"The vicar knows of only one occasion when somebody was up in the bell-chamber legitimately this year," George said, when they had been through everything. "That was in late May, when a swarm of bees invaded. Bees get in wherever they think they will. Anyhow, they moved in among the woodwork there, and if the Reverend Stephen didn't want 'em, at least he knew of some who did."

"'A swarm of bees in May . . . '", murmured Moon sententiously.

"I know! 'Worth a load of hay.' And we're talking in Middlehope terms now. Well, the leading bass, Joe Llewelyn, is a fanatical bee-keeper, and wins prizes with his honey all over Britain. So Joe moved in to take the swarm. Nobody'd laid claim to it, it seems they may well have been wild bees. Joe came twice, once to size up the situation, and the second time with a skip, and an assistant to help him. And the assistant was Bossie Jarvis. I can well believe that if there was anything out of the ordinary going on, Bossie'd be in on it. Joe's got no complaints. He got his bees, and Bossie was first-class as aide-de-camp. Those two seem to be the only people who have been up there with those two chests of magazines this year. Joe is sure both chests were left tidily closed when they came away. The one is more or less empty, anyhow, just a few rotting organ scores. Joe is particularly sure because Bossie, when not fully occupied, was poking about curiously in the other chest, the full one. He'd never be able to resist any reading matter, anyhow, the odder the better. But they left everything as they found it when they came down with the swarm."

"So that accounts for one person who disturbed the layers of dust," agreed Moon placidly. "But in May."

"And now it's October, and somebody's been at them very recently. And Rainbow is an antiquarian, but hardly likely to be after *The Gentleman's Magazine*, even for seventeen-some-odd. So if it was Rainbow, what *was* he after? And why should he expect to find it there?

105

And *did* he find it? And above all, can it possibly have been something worth killing him for?"

★ ★ ★

By the time they adjourned to pick up some cigarettes at the village shop before closing time, and snatch a pint and a sandwich at the 'Gun Dog', forensic had rung with reports on the matter found in Rainbow's head-wound, and on that detected on the sliver of voussoir that had fractured his skull. The same stone-debris, the same species of moss, the same blood. The victim's finger-nails had also provided specimens of all but the blood. No doubt about it, that was where he had died, and that was how he had died. Only who, and why, remained to he documented.

"Which first?" wondered George, stretching lengthily after hours of sitting. "Motive? My God, there's no getting out of range of one motive, up here, is there? And yet ninety-nine-point-nine per cent of the time Middlehope is madly sane, if you'll permit the paradox. They know this sort of solution only promotes a far worse problem. I don't say they wouldn't — I just say they wouldn't without total safeguards for all the valley. And we also have a most equivocal lady, with a trail of admirers a mile long. And she surprisingly at home here, where he insulated himself totally. Perhaps he did everywhere? There are people who are chronically strangers here!"

"Sad, that!" said Sergeant Moon. "But what can you do, if they do the sealing? We've got nothing from the solicitors yet. Never take for granted the 'Cui bono'."

"I'll see Bowes in person tomorrow morning," said George. "Do you feel as dry as I do?"

"Like a lime-kiln. And I'm out of Woodbines. Mind if we stop in at Gwen's?"

Gwen was Mrs Owen Lloyd, keeper of the shop, and mother of Toffee Bill.

"A good idea," said George. "At closing time there might he something interesting to hear." For closing time did not hurry in the village. Trade ceased, but social exchanges frequently continued for another half-hour. And there was a sensation to be discussed today.

The shop was located on a corner, an enlarged house-window and an old, leaning roof above it, the usual invaluable local shop that has everything you're ever going to need in an emergency, from gumstrip to TCP, and frozen peas to fresh eggs. It was as immaculate and brisk as all such genuinely professional shops are, and as informal, an exchange-point for news and gossip, a first-aid post for local protection, sending out feelers towards isolated old people unaccountably not seen for some days, delivering without benefit of fee where there was need, advising where regulation forms frightened intelligent but direct folk out of their normal routine. Its compact space of freezer and cases and shelves was everything anybody needed of modernity, without the gimmicks. And Gwen was a farmer's daughter, fresh as new milk, large, fair and kind.

Miss de la Pole was standing at the counter when they entered, in the act of lighting one of the small cheroots she had just been buying. "I shouldn't worry," she was saying comfortably, in her ripe baritone, "the child's too close to it, that's all. He just can't digest it, it isn't that he really cares. Give him a week or two, and he'll have forgotten all about it. The man wasn't likeable, you know, nobody can blame the boys for not liking him." She turned and recognised the police entering. "Why, hullo, George! We were just talking about this affair. Hullo, Jack, nice to know you're standing by. I must say, it's a shake-up for us all."

"It is," agreed Moon heartily. "Here yesterday and gone today. It makes you take stock."

"I've been doing that for some time," she assured him drily. "At my age, one does. You're just a youngster, Jack. And then, I must have disliked him about as violently as anyone could, and that does make one take stock, as you put it."

"You didn't, by any chance, make away with him, did you?" asked George mildly.

"No, sorry, George, I don't really have the resolution, you know. I might dream about it, I'm unlikely ever to do it. In any case, I'm probably one of the last to see him alive, and he was mobile at the time, so I didn't get the chance. I happened to look out of the window before I drew the curtains, last night, round about a quarter to twelve, and I saw him driving towards the gates, on his way home."

Wonder of wonders, she was one of those whom the grapevine reached only vaguely, because in her aristocratic solitude she merely received, never queried. She knew Rainbow was dead, but had not acquired the details. Doubtless she knew he had been found broken under the church tower, but the time was unknown to her, and the spectacle of a man driving home at a time when he had almost certainly been dead presented her with no problems. Here was one who could have confessed to his murder with absolute security, her guilt disproved within ten minutes.

"Oh, really?" said George cautiously. "Coming down from the head of the valley, was he? Which car was he using?"

"The little sports job." Her voice was faintly disapproving. The Aston Martin was not what she would have expected of Rainbow. "Very handsome," she admitted, "as a work of art. Not his style, would you think? There was something so — orthodox and cautious — about him."

Well, that was something definite, She knew the little sports job too well to he mistaken, and she had the incisive mind that is always scrupulous in reporting and accurate in timing. She had something else, too, the shrewdness to note their very slight stiffening, and the brief glance they had exchanged, and that was all it took to make her look again at what she had seen and said, and wonder exactly what had taken Rainbow up the valley towards Wales after choir practice, and above all, what had taken him back to the church at nearly midnight, since that was where he had been found. From that it was but a step to pondering whether the Aston Martin had been left in its garage or taken out again, and whether, in fact, it had actually been Rainbow driving it . . .

A remote and thoughtful stillness took possession of Miss de la Pole's noble countenance, out of which concerned and steely eyes studied George and Sergeant Moon, and drew private conclusions.

"His missus chose the Aston, I fancy," said Sergeant Moon with a face of bovine innocence, and paid for his Woodbines. "They both drove it, though. Thanks, Gwen, love!"

He led the way out, and George was aware, as he was, of the deep silence of the two women left behind them in the shop. Moon was grinning.

"Whose side are you on?" George wondered tolerantly.

"Well, be interesting to see what results, won't it? You going to get that pint and bite before you go and tackle the lady?"

"I am," said George, and set course for the 'Gun Dog'. "I'm going to need it!"

4

COLIN BARRON'S car was out on the semi-circle of meticulously-raked gravel, a green SAAB, very dark and sleek and reticent; and Colin Barron was sitting in the small drawing-room with a whisky glass in his hand and restrained and chivalrous concern on his brow, looking very correct in the role of a would-be beau come to commiserate with his intended on her sudden bereavement. A very complex role indeed, but he was managing rather well. No doubt the discreet flowers in a vase on the coffee table, lilac and purple tinted, had come from him, the delicate hint of mourning combined with the suggestion of a tentative love-gift. He was a very presentable fellow, and no doubt they would make a handsome couple, if it ever came to that, but he wasn't presuming on his hopes. When George appeared, Colin rose politely, greeted the visitor with an intelligent acceptance of his official status, as opposed to the social contact they had occasionally shared, cast a wistful glance at Barbara to see what she desired, and read her wishes with resigned good-humour.

"I just dropped in to say what one does say in this sort of crisis. Not that it can do much for anyone, but at least it goes to show one is there in readiness. Barbara knows she has only to call on me." He looked at her again, but got no encouragement. "She doesn't feel any need of me now, and I don't feel any need to stand around to defend her against you, Superintendent. She's as good as nodding me out of the door. And since she knows I'll be back for less than a nod. I'm going."

"It was nice of you to come. Colin." said Barbara, "and I do appreciate it. I'm sure I shall need your help, if it comes to selling up, but it's early days yet to think of that. But thanks, anyhow. I'll be in touch."

"You'll be fine," said the young man rather ruefully. "Don't I know it! But call me on any pretext, any time. I'll be glad."

He knew the place well enough by now to be allowed to depart unescorted, and doubtless he would be back just as informally if she neglected to call him. The silence closed in after his going.

"Do sit down," said Barbara, eyeing George somewhat quizzically, and herself set the example. "Whatever it is, you're never unwelcome, you know. I'd offer you a drink. But I have the feeling you wouldn't take it, and that would be rather sad. So you speak first, and then we'll see where the clues lead."

She had plainly been relaxing after a bath when Barron arrived. The glow was still on her, she was without make-up, and swathed in a loose gown of heavy Indian cotton in a sumptuous flower-print in red and greens on black, with a padded yoke and voluminous sleeves. Her hair was a cloud about head and shoulders, coiled and moist from steam. She had a marvellously serene beauty. Maybe this was the first time Barbara had been alone, in the sense of her own person and responsible only to herself, for a long time.

"I just wondered," said George mildly.

"if you'd like to amend your story about how you spent yesterday evening."

"I wouldn't really like to," said Barbara reasonably, and still smiling with that distant composure in which he had so little part, "but I can see I'd better." And the smile suddenly warmed into genuine intimacy. There was mischief in it, and sympathy. She was positively inviting him to connive at a friendly compromise.

Naturally, Moon's guess had been right. Miss de la Pole had telephoned her as soon as the police were out of sight. Not taking sides, simply informing a possibly threatened neighbour of the accidental information lodged against her. How marvellous was the working of the conscience of Middlehope! And how simply, almost inadvertently, it had absorbed within itself this blatantly alien body. George respected the instinct that worked within so idiosyncratic a community, but reserved his options. Even Middlehope could be wrong.

"Then suppose you tell me," he said, "as if we hadn't been over this ground before, exactly how you spent yesterday evening."

"I did lie to you," she said, quite softly and serenely. "I told you I was home all the evening, waiting for Arthur. I wasn't. I was here until he went off to practice, and he'd told me he was staying late, and I was here cooped up on my own, and that's something I don't always choose to be. About nine I took my car and went out for a drive. It was a nice, mild night, I knew he wouldn't be back for some time, and I felt like being out and alone. And frankly, I didn't care if he got back first. It wouldn't have troubled him at all, you know. I had functions, and I performed them. He wasn't worried about what I did on the side. I went quite a long way. It can't have been far off midnight when I got back. He wasn't home. I took it then that he wasn't coming, but he had his keys, anyhow. I went to bed. And the rest is just as I told you." She reached for her drink with a hand steady as a rock. "And that's all," she said, and looked him firmly in the eye.

"You mean you were driving round for a matter of perhaps two and a half hours, alone?" said George mildly.

"I suppose I must have been."

"Nothing else to tell me?"

"Nothing."

And whatever he might think of that, it seemed to be agreed that she had driven in at the gates here at about a quarter to midnight, well after the probable time of her husband's death, though not after the limit of possibility. And from the opposite direction. Driving someone else back out of the danger zone before returning home herself? The timing made it possible that she had guilty knowledge, even that she could have assisted at Rainbow's demise, or at least connived at it, even if it seemed unlikely that she managed it alone. Rainbow had seemed to value her simply as one of the most advantageous of his investments, but there were plenty of other men who showed every sign of putting a very different value upon her. Which of them, if any, could she have been running home, or at least to a place of safety, up the valley?

"And you didn't call in anywhere for a drink?"

"No. Nor drop in on any friend. Nor even call for a paper of chips," she said with a fleeting smile, "though I do remember Charlie had been frying. No, I didn't stop to speak to a soul, and I doubt if anyone noticed me passing." She made no mention, naturally, of Miss de la Pole; she understood the rules of the game by instinct.

"It won't do, you know," said George simply.

"It will have to, won't it?" she said just as simply, and smiled at him.

He was sure then that there was someone else involved, and Barbara had no intention of letting him — it had to be him! — be drawn into a case. Not only would she deny his existence, she would probably warn him off, whoever he was, from coming near her until this affair blew over. Did that mean there was any guilt involved? Not necessarily. Just that she was well aware there could be suspicion of guilt.

"All right," said George equably. "That's your story. If you ever decide to change it, call me."

She went out to the forecourt with him. There was a chill wind blowing between the sheltering trees. "Do go in," said George, remembering she was fresh from the bath. "You shouldn't risk catching cold."

She gazed at him for a moment with an unreadable face, and then suddenly smiled at him, and turned and went back into the house without a word, and closed the door softly between them.

* * *

Rainbow's solicitors were a Comerbourne firm, a fanfare of four resounding names, not one of which survived in the company. The man George wanted was a Mr Bowes, middle-aged, thin and spry. Yes, he held Rainbow's will, and yes, he fully understood the significance it might hold for the police investigation. *'Cui bono'* is still sound sense. Until after the inquest and the release of the body for burial, he remained the sole custodian of Rainbow's testamentary dispositions, but he made no bones about divulging them to the officer in charge.

"It's a very concise affair. There are small legacies to his assistants in both shops. Abbot's Bale House is left to

120

his wife, with all its contents. But the residual legatee, who gets his businesses, all his holdings in banks and stocks, the lot, is the manageress of his Birmingham shop. A Miss Isobel Lavery."

It was a shock, and yet it probably should not have been. The partnership with Barbara, on any but the most superficial examination, bore all the marks of a business arrangement, a mutual benefit alliance.

"And I take it that the residue will amount to a pretty considerable fortune? Judging by his way of living — and I never heard that he gave anyone the impression of being a bad financial risk?"

"Anything but," agreed Mr Bowes frankly. "There'll be not far short of a quarter of a million to come to Miss Lavery."

Enough to provide an added incentive, supposing a wife who repented of her bargain felt the urge to break free; always supposing, also, of course, that she didn't know she wasn't going to get it! But undoubtedly by the same token Miss Lavery represented another possibility to be taken into account. And if she occupied so confidential a place in Rainbow's life as to come in for the lion's share of his property, the odds were that she, at least, not having the security of a wife, would need to know very well what was in his will. Businesswomen can usually take care of their own interests. She might, of course, be the exception.

"Have you met Miss Lavery?"

"Once or twice, on Mr Rainbow's business. No doubt you'll have to see her. You'll be able to make your own assessment." Clearly he had made his, if he wasn't willing to share it. "I haven't yet been in touch with her, but I believe Mrs Rainbow has. In view of what's happened, I suppose she may have decided to close the shop. You'd better have her home address, too, just in case."

As it turned out, however, Miss Isobel Lavery took a sternly business-like view even of death. The shop in Birmingham, a narrow but expensive frontage leading far back through several well-furnished rooms, proved to be open for business as usual. A young girl at a fragile Regency desk came forward to enquire his interest, and opened her eyes wide when he asked for the manageress. She vanished into the mysterious rear regions, and came back a few minutes later to lead him into a small, plain office. The elaborations were kept for the showrooms, though this austere workroom was elegant enough in its own way.

Miss Lavery could have been called many things, handsome, decorative, even sumptuous, but not elegant. She was a tall, full-breasted blonde with an excellent figure, and a great casque of lacquered hair in pale, silvery gold. Light blue eyes artistically shadowed with darker blue gazed coolly and shrewdly out of a clear-featured face that erred only slightly on the side of coldness and hardness. She had, he thought, added a few funereal touches of black jewellery and a knotted georgette scarf to the black dress she habitually wore in the shop. She was not broken-hearted, but she was observing the conventions of bereavement. There was even a handkerchief, large, silken and expensive, and bordered two inches deep with black, grey and silver lace, deployed ready on her desk.

It was easy to see why, though

for this setting and this purpose she was manifestly right, she would have been hopelessly wrong as hostess to the eccentric aristocracy of Middlehope, and châtelaine of the country house at Abbot's Bale. Rainbow had believed in horses for courses.

"Yes, Mrs Rainbow telephoned me with the news yesterday afternoon," she said. Nearly all the Brummie had been ironed out of her voice, but not quite all; she was of the city. "It was a terrible shock, as you can imagine. I thought he would not have wanted me to close the shop. He was completely professional. If you invite the public to do business with you, you must remain available, or they have a legitimate complaint. I wanted to do what he would have wished."

She answered questions readily. No, she had had no communication with Mr Rainbow on the day of his death, or the day previous to it, and she knew of nothing that could possibly shed light on what had happened to him. The last time she had spoken to him, by telephone, was two days earlier, when they had discussed the lots to be bid for at a

124

forthcoming sale, and she had carried out his suggestions and bought the pieces he wanted. There had been no suggestion of anything unusual or disturbing in the conversation or his manner. The last time she had seen him was a week before that, when he had come down and stayed in town overnight, and they had had dinner together.

Ten days might be quite a long abstention. Had Barbara taken it for granted that he had gone into town to join his mistress, the night he died? It made sense, in the light of her reactions.

"Thank you, Miss Lavery, you've been very helpful," said George truthfully, when she had poured out her willing confidences, and wondered almost convincingly what was to happen to the business now, and whether Mrs Rainbow would wish things to continue in the old way. "I'm sure you're right to keep the place open and functioning, and wait for instructions. Your position can hardly be threatened in any way." That was bait, and in spite of herself she rose to it. He saw the brief, cool flame of triumph in her eyes, before she reached for the handkerchief and hid them behind it. She knew, all right, who owned the business from now on.

"Just a formality," he said, remaining seated when she was sure he was about to rise and go, "I'm sure you won't mind telling me what your own movements were on Thursday night?"

After the almost reverent tone of their interview, she should have been visibly shaken by this sudden descent to earth, but she was not even ruffled. She had expected it, and she knew why. Oh, yes, she knew how much her hold on Rainbow had been worth, and she was prepared now for the resultant enquiry. And though anything she said would have to be checked, he knew then that it would be time wasted. She knew she was in the clear, and nobody and nothing could get between her and that quarter of a million.

"I understand," she said, "that you have to ask everyone connected with him. I was at home all the evening, after I left the shop at six. I had a little bridge party, we meet on Thursdays at seven when we're all free, at each flat in turn, and this time it was at my place. I'll give you all the names, I know you have to check." And she did; two of them women, single like herself, the fourth a man in attendance on one of the girls; and George knew that they would check out without blemish, as in the event they did. "We broke up about eleven-thirty. We all live fairly close, you see."

He saw, and more than she was recommending to his sight. He saw a woman quite prepared to stake her body, somewhat resignedly, against future profits, but rather preferring, if truth were told, the small local bridge four, and the cosy coffee-evenings in city flats, without penalty. Now she could be both respectable and rich.

She went out with him to the street, which was a concession that betrayed her unease, not about her own immunity, which was absolute, but about something more subtle and vulnerable, her whole new situation. She thought she was on the verge of bliss, of fulfilment in riches, and yet some hidden part of her was nervous of the change. In anticipation it was unshadowed gain, now on the threshold she was seeing those little bridge parties shrivelling into ashes, the old friends dropping off, the horizon abruptly extended into frightful distances of challenge? Or was this dread he felt in her only that something might yet loom between her and Rainbow's money?

"I suppose there's bound to be some delay about probate, in the circumstances." she said almost wincingly, at parting. "But there won't be any serious difficulties, will there? I mean, I have the business to manage in the meantime, I ought to know how I stand as soon as possible."

"I'm sure everything will proceed normally," said George with resigned tolerance. "Whatever dispositions Mr Rainbow made about his property will be observed. Subject, of course, to the obvious innocence of all legatees in the circumstances leading to his death. The inquest shouldn't be a great obstacle." He could feel her subdued tension sending out ripples through the air, and he understood the passion with which the hardworking poor — for what else was she, with inflation at this level? — look forward to almost unimaginable wealth.

He didn't blame her very much. Pretty obviously she had provided with very limited reward what was now to be repaid in full at last.

But when he took his leave of her and returned to the local police yard where he had left his car, he was wondering at every step whether she was going to be glad or sorry when she received and realised in full the blessing and the burden of her inheritance.

★ ★ ★

"Inquest opens Monday," said George to Sergeant Moon, across a table littered with files. It was evening, and they were preparing to hand back the parish hall and transfer their enquiries to headquarters in Comerbourne. "We can take it as far as murder in one go, or ask for an adjournment and keep them guessing. The Chief Constable will back us whatever we do, luckily, he's local, and knows what will happen if he brings the Yard in. He doesn't want border warfare on his hands, any more than we do. I'm going to clam up for a week, and hang on to the options. Miss Lavery will be on hot bricks a week longer, but it won't hurt her."

"And she's clean." mused Moon, almost regretfully, for Miss Lavery was not of the valley, and therefore to a certain extent expendable.

"In her own person, absolutely. She was where she said she was, and there are three witnesses to prove it. Besides, she isn't the type."

"Too moral?" enquired Moon, interested.

"Too limited, unless some other person did it for her. There could, I suppose, be some other fellow around who wants Miss Lavery, and whom she, if truth were told, can't help preferring to Rainbow. But I suspect all her familiars will turn out to play bridge for low stakes, and give little coffee-parties. Still, you never know. There could be a cheerful, extrovert, over-sexed wholesale butcher around, who likes blondes and resents rivals. Keep an open mind, Jack."

"My mind is always open," said Moon truthfully. "Murder, which unquestionably we have on our hands, requires a motive, and in spite of all the modern complications, the main motives for killing are money and sex. Here, let's face it, we've got a third, local solidarity in the face of an indigestible threat. I know it, you know it. I wouldn't rule it out. Still — Rainbow had money, and plenty of it, and his wife has sex, and plenty of that, too. By the way, I was interested enough to do some checking this afternoon. She *is* his wife. I did wonder. She's got her marriage lines, all right. Nineteen when she married him. I reckon that makes a sort of sense. Barbara Cranmer. Father died in 'fifty-seven of long-delayed illness arising from war injuries. Mother ran a flower shop, not very prosperous, not very efficient, and Barbara helped in it. I bet he was buying flowers for Miss Lavery when he clapped eyes on Barbara."

"I marvel," said George mildly, "how you manage to extract life stories in an afternoon. Where is mother now?"

"Died, two years ago. Barbara's on her own. Since the marriage mother's been living in a very nice residential hotel on the south coast. She died of leukemia in a very expensive nursing home. Oh, yes, I've been busy. Still, here we still are, stuck with money and sex. And a set of circumstances, of course."

"Quite remarkable circumstances, when you come to think about it. Somebody — potentially Rainbow himself — had certainly been poking around privately among the junk up there in the tower. Very recently, possibly the night he was killed. And Rainbow was a knowledgeable chap in his own line, with a nose for buried treasure. So one of his colleagues and rivals assured me, the night he had his house-warming party. Where he goes, this lad said, it's worthwhile following, and taking a good sniff around. So had he sniffed out something profitable here in Abbot's Bale? More precisely, up in the church tower? He took precautions, apparently, to have the place on his own that night. Something really sensational? Worth following him for? Worth killing him for, perhaps? If so, what was it? What *is* it?"

"I'll tell you this," said Moon promptly, "if he thought he was on to something good there, he never said a word to the vicar or to anyone else. He was keeping it strictly to himself, all right. Looks as though somebody else had got a whiff of what was going on, and was keeping an eye on him accordingly. Two of 'em met up there in the tower."

Two of them had indeed met in the tower, to deadly effect. The forensic boys had isolated three sets of prints, two of which had definitely reached the leads, one of them Rainbow's. The second was a long, narrow foot, with an even, springy tread that argued a younger man, with unmangled feet, probably accustomed always to well-made, expensive shoes, certainly wearing new and good leather soles when these prints were salvaged from the leads. A third set of prints could be traced as far as that model impression on the lowest stair of the bell-chamber staircase, but was not distinguishable any higher. Cracked old shoes, trodden askew to favour a probable bunion; an older man's foot. Not Joe Llewelyn's, either, nowhere near so big and a good many years older.

"He's only been dead approximately forty-five hours," said Sergeant Moon. sensibly reducing everything to its true proportion.

"And we have at least moved, and we have a Chief who'll stay with us, even when he gets nervous. So come on, let's get this paper-work into shape for Monday, and trust the Coroner to have a pulse, too." The coroner's officer was a second cousin of Sergeant Moon, shared his kinsman's sensitivity to local feeling, and exercised a powerful influence over his elderly and irascible but timorous chief. "Hand me that file," sighed George, clearing the table before him, "and get Barnes in here. I'm going for an adjournment."

★ ★ ★

Bossie Jarvis had a music lesson on Saturday evenings, and his piano teacher lived in Comerford, down the valley. Comerford was a sometime idyllic village, now beset with invading population from the Midland conurbation, with supermarkets and car-parks, and all the ills of modern living, though it retained a superb setting rimmed with rising hills growing grim and purple towards the west. Bossie took a bus from home about seven o'clock, and trudged along with his music-case to Miss Griffith's house in Church Street, to embroil himself in mortal combat with her very nice grand for half an hour. He enjoyed the battle, but would never have admitted it. He had his eye on the organ, some day, and dreamed of letting loose those earth-shaking stops, and curbing them at will or letting them split the world apart. And his teacher, though unmarried and therefore an Old Maid, was no more than twenty-three, extremely pretty and spirited, and fought him amicably over the keyboard in a fashion which sent him away fulfilled like a lover. If, of course, he had had the slightest notion how a satisfied lover feels, or, for that matter, an unsatisfied one. All Bossie knew was that he went off finally to catch his minibus home, all the company would furnish at that time of night, feeling fat, and fed, and boss.

But this Saturday evening, though events proceeded exactly as usual, Bossie was not entirely present. He played grimly, but with half his mind on other matters. He had spent an hour of the afternoon in earnest council with his allies and fellow-conspirators, and they had debated anxiously how they should behave in this new and unforeseen situation. Rainbow was dead, and they were in possession of certain knowledge which might be of importance to the police enquiry. Yet they could not possibly tell what they knew. They would even have liked to, to be rid of the responsibility, but in the circumstances it was impossible. They were all firmly agreed about that.

"If it was only us," said Ginger, "we could tell. But it isn't, and we can't. Anyhow, we don't know all that much. What somebody else tells you isn't evidence. You're the only one who really has anything to tell, and we don't think you should, and you don't think so, either, and if you agree we've got to stay mum, that's what we'll do."

And since that was exactly what they had instinctively done up to now, it was the easiest thing to go on behaving in the same way. In any case, there was nothing else for it. That did not, however, make them any happier about it. Even Bossie felt less assured of his rightness than usual, though he suppressed the heretical thought firmly.

The minibus made a slower journey than the ordinary daily service buses, since the driver went round in a series of short detours to drop a number of regular passengers at isolated farms on the way. It was past nine o'clock when it turned about by the Church at Abbot's Bale, and set down Bossie, the last of the load. From there he had a ten-minute walk home, by a side-road not much frequented at night, since it led only to two or three scattered homes before climbing out of the valley over a ridge to the south, narrowing considerably as it went. He knew every yard of it, having walked it regularly every day for years, the darkness did not worry him in the least. It was the almost moonless part of the month, and clouded over into the bargain, and once out of the village lights and away from visible windows it was very dark indeed. The hedges were high, the occasional field-drive came abruptly, but the road was wide enough here for two cars to pass.

Somewhere ahead an engine was heard briefly, the sound emerging and retreating with a curve of the road; it occurred to him at the time that it had the same smooth note of the car that had driven past in this direction just as he got off the bus, but cars were not among the things Bossie studied with any diligence, things mechanical being of no interest to him apart from the mechanics of the organ. Somebody from over the ridge going home, probably, or a visitor to one of the farms.

A faint pallor on the left was, of course, the white gate of the Croppings drive. Just round the next curve, on the right, came the narrow turning into the lane to the Lyons' farm, shrouded between tall hedges and rising very sharply from the road. Bob Lyons had a way of coasting down that slope at speed, and sailing out silently to the indignation of the unwary. Sergeant Moon had often warned him about it.

That was exactly what the car lying in wait there did now, just after Bossie had passed the end of the lane. Only the otherwise profound silence of the night warned him. He had already tuned out his own light footfalls, and infinitely small though the betraying sounds were, they came to him clearly, if at first inexplicably. The slight crunch of gravel on a hard lane surface, under tyres, the whip and slither of untrimmed leaves along a wing, very soft indeed and yet seeming to bear down upon him at frightful speed. He felt the rushing displacement of air, and sensed a heavy projectile hurtling out upon him.

Instinct did well by Bossie. The sudden gleam of lights cast his shadow on the road ahead, and he realised that the car, engine now running, was sweeping into a right turn after him. To leap to the left would have been to remain in its path a couple of seconds longer. Bossie flung his music-case away from him, and leaped to the right, instead, aiming high into the thick verdure of the autumn hedgerow, clear of the road.

He all but made it to safety, his hands spread to grasp even at thorn to haul himself higher out of range. The front wing of the car struck him glancingly on the left hip, and flung him sprawling aside, short of his aim but clear of the wheels. He hit the road with arms spread, which partially saved his face, but even so his head struck with some force, and his cheek slid jarringly along the tarmac. He lay winded and bruised and half-stunned, feeling the grain of the road coarse as boulders, and groping with wincing finger-tips around him, without the power to prise himself up from the ground and run.

Dazedly he wondered what the red glow was, that was very gradually growing brighter and nearer. Then he knew. The car that had hit him had halted some yards ahead, but no one had got out to run and see what damage had been done. What he was watching with sick fascination, was the rear lights backing gently towards him. Not directly towards him, rather away to the left, carefully and slowly, drawing level with him now. All this time he must have been staring straight at the rear number-plate, only there weren't any numbers, or any letters, either, only a blank. And the rear wheels were sliding softly past his left shoulder, down to his hip, down towards his knee . . .

He broke clear of his daze in a frantic heave, and tried to raise himself, and nothing would work, nothing at all, and the car was creeping back, half a minute more and it would be clear of him and behind him, and then he knew what was going to happen, and he scrabbled frantically with nerveless hands and ungovernable toes to scuttle away into the grass, and knew he wasn't moving so much as an inch.

"Now, look here, God," raged Bossie's submerged Christian innocence, somewhere deep inside him, "this isn't fair, you can't just stand there! It isn't bloody good enough!" He was accustomed to pray as candidly and robustly as he argued with his father, and in a comparable emergency he would probably have sworn at his father, too. It was now or never, wasn't it?

The lights of an approaching car swept an arc above him, rounding a curve still some hundred yards back, darkened momentarily, and returned in a steady glow, though still with the hulk of a hedge between. Seconds, and they would be here, and the car by Bossie's side had not yet cleared his body, and had no time now to straighten out behind him. The engine throbbed, the forward leap at speed tore the long twigs of the hedge swishing after it, and the long grass surged and strained forward to follow. The rear lights reappeared large and bright, and soared away, diminishing, until they vanished in red pin-points round the next corner, accelerating all the way.

Bossie let his breath spill out of him like blood, rested his grazed cheek in his arm, and waited trustingly to be salvaged. He was barely half-conscious when the approaching car, travelling with the timeless benignity of the happy and well-disposed, braked sharply and drew up well short of the spot where he lay, and two people came tumbling out, concerned and competent, to pick up the pieces.

5

THE telephone rang just as George was clearing up for the evening, with every intention of putting his feet up for the few hours remaining, and renewing his perspective on the case by seeing it at greater distance and through Bunty's eyes. He should have known better than to expect anything so pleasurable.

"Glad you're still there, sir." It was Barnes on the line. "I thought I might catch the sergeant, at any rate. We've got a rather rum thing here, hit-and-run, up in the southerly road, where the Lyons drive comes in. People in a following car picked up the victim, and the lady's gone in with the kid to the hospital, called the ambulance and all. Reason I thought it just might be something for you, the lad who got knocked down is one of the choirboys, and it was Mrs Rainbow who came along in the Aston Martin and salvaged him.

Maybe I'm reaching rather far, but unless coincidence is working overtime, there ought to be some connection. Anyhow, I thought you should know, right away. It's Sam Jarvis's lad. Not to worry too much, from all I gather he just got knocked sideways and shocked and grazed, no serious injuries, he'll be all right."

"Thank God for that!" said George. "Have his people been notified? Where have they taken him? Comerbourne General?"

"That's right. Mrs Rainbow said she'd call them from the hospital as soon as they got there."

"Good, but I'll have a word with Sam, too. Who was it travelling with Mrs Rainbow? People, you said."

"That's right. Mr Swayne was with her. He stood by and took care of the boy while she went to call the ambulance. Now the lads are on the spot he's taken the Aston Martin and followed on down to the hospital to collect her."

Well, well! Not Colin Barron, not John Stubbs, none of her old circle, but our own Willie the Twig, thought George. Heading out, not homeward, with Barbara, after nine o'clock at night. That little flame of interest at the house-warming didn't just flicker out when they were apart. Two people worse-suited, on the face of it, it would be hard to find. Willie the impervious and self-sufficient recluse, married to a forest and never likely to want a divorce, and Barbara the sophisticate and hostess, out of her world when out of the city. On the face of it!

"Right, we'll be out there and have a look." George hung up, and reached for his coat. "Come on, Jack, we seem to have what may or may not be a further development."

He told him about it in the car, on the way to the quiet stretch of road where the farm drive swept down into the highway. It was considerably less dark now, with a policeman standing by to flag down any stray traffic, and lights surrounding the area where the approximate position of Bossie's form had been chalked out on the tarmac. After fine, dry weather the surface showed nothing of wheel-tracks.

"But the hedges in the lane want brushing back," said the uniformed sergeant in charge, turning his lights on the thick greenery. "There's been a car backed in there on to the edge of the grass, see, backed in just far enough to be out of sight, the tracks go no further. Courting couple, most likely, finding a nice private place and reckoning there isn't going to be much farm traffic this late. It looks as if that was the car that came out and hit him, luckily the knock just threw him clear. There might be traces on the wing, if ever we find the right car, but they could be very slight, nothing to attract attention." There were ends of grasses and a few small twigs brushed out from the hedge where the car had stood, and scattered a yard or two after its progress, obviously freshly severed.

"Won't get any tyre-marks out of that lot," said Sergeant Moon thoughtfully. "In the grass it's just a furrow, and as soon as it touches the lane surface it vanishes. Too hard and too dry."

"And the other car? Mrs Rainbow's? I hear she went with the boy in the ambulance." That was nice of her, and for some reason not at all surprising.

"Yes, sir. That one was standing back

here ten yards short of where the boy was lying, when we got here, heading away from Abbot's Bale, over the ridge. Mr Swayne stayed to give us a statement, and then followed down to the hospital. Everything bears out their account. They heard a car start up, fast, before they came into this stretch. By the time they did, all they saw were the rear-lights just vanishing at the end of this longish straight. They were driving quite slowly themselves, and have first-rate headlights, or they might have driven over the boy, he was in dark school clothes, and this surface eats light."

"Thanks," said George, "we'll get to them as soon as we've checked how Bossie's doing."

"Accident?" wondered Moon, as they drove down the valley towards Comerford.

"Apparently. Even probably. But there's always the odd possibility . . . "

"She'll have contacted his parents," said Moon comfortably, "the minute she had something officially reassuring to say. And ten to one she'll stay around until the docs have been over him and voted him sound as a bell."

His view of the alien female was illuminating, as though some false outlines in the portrait of Barbara were beginning to melt and run, and reassemble into a different pattern. "And if she's still there," he went on positively, "you'll find Willie the Twig sitting waiting for her, with all the patience in the world."

★ ★ ★

Barbara's Aston Martin was standing alone in the public car park attached to one flank of the Comerbourne General Hospital, when they reached it just before ten o'clock, and Willie the Twig, in his normal leather-elbowed, thorny tweeds and creaseless, comfortable slacks, was sitting on one of the synthetic hide benches in the reception area, one long leg crossed over the other, and a very old *Country Life* in his lap, exchanging occasional sallies with the nurse at the reception desk and the aide on the switchboard, but for the most part turning the pages of his magazine with imperturbable patience and a certain startled interest, perhaps viewing the prices of houses at five years' remove, and wondering at the way they had ballooned since. His spiky fair hair was on end in all directions, which was normality itself, and the elongated, fleshless image he projected, from natural-Shetland, polo-collared throat to narrow classical brogues, was, if one stood back and took a fresh look at the whole, elegant in the extreme. Elegance of body and mind might well count with Barbara. Money could not match it, as money could not provide it.

He looked up when George entered, with Sergeant Moon at his elbow. His thick, reddish-blond brows shot up, and hid bright grey eyes radiated mild surprise and pleasure.

"Well, hullo, have they dragged you in on this, too? I call that excess of zeal, you know. The kid's going to be as right as rain, all he's got is a grazed cheek, a bunch of bruises on one hip, and a bad case of precautionary sedation. I'd have given him a shot of brandy and put him to bed for about twenty hours, and he'd have come out fighting."

"From all we know of him," agreed George drily, "he probably will. Is Mrs Rainbow still in there with them?"

"Try and get her out until she knows the score. His folks are on the way, did they tell you? We called them, they know he's OK. The chap who hit him took off like a rocket when he heard us coming. We wondered what had bitten somebody up there ahead of us. I reckon he was going to have a look what damage he'd done, but when he heard us coming he didn't want to be there to answer for it."

"Lucky you were driving so circumspectly," said George, with only the mildest irony, for Willie's volcanic but expert driving was notorious.

"I wasn't driving, George. And we were in no hurry." Willie the Twig had a gentle line in irony, too.

The nurse on reception, who was young, and not a local girl, hovered suggestively, primly waiting for the newcomer to state his business and credentials, but she was forestalled by the appearance of an elderly sister who knew Superintendent Felse very well from many and varied contacts. Sailing before her, in a burst of brightness that cried aloud gloriously against all the hospital white, came Barbara Rainbow. She wore a long, narrow skirt slit to the knee, in a deep petunia colour, and an embroidered mandarin coat of thin, padded silk, and her hair was knotted in a bunch of curls on top of her head, and fastened with a tall jet comb. Anything further removed from widow's weeds it would have been impossible to imagine; maybe that was the reason for the get-up. And here sat Willie the Twig in his usual country suiting, as perfectly content with her brilliance as she was with his casualness. She saw George, and smiled radiantly. She looked fulfilled and roused and happy, whether for private reasons of her own and Willie's, or simply because she had risen to an unexpected occasion with decision and success, and felt all the better for it.

"You don't want to see the patient tonight, do you?" said the sister promptly. "It wouldn't do you a bit of good, he's sedated, and in any case the doctor won't let anybody try to question him yet."

"I did come with that intention," George admitted, "but I'd already gathered it wouldn't be allowed. As long as he's all right I don't suppose leaving it until tomorrow morning will make much difference. You are keeping him overnight?"

"Doctor thought it wise, in case of delayed shock, but if you ask me he's pretty tough. Dazed, but there doesn't seem to be any concussion. But we're keeping him in to be on the safe side."

"And there's nothing really damaged? Nothing to worry about?"

She detailed Bossie's few abrasions and bruises placidly, and guaranteed his generally sound condition.

"Did he have anything to say when you got him in? He usually has plenty, if he was conscious I can't imagine him being silent."

She thought about that seriously, as if something unusual had just been brought to her notice. "Now you come to mention it, we hardly got a cheep out of him, except answers to 'does that hurt?' and that sort of thing. Oh, and he did say he'd lost his music-case, and Mrs

Rainbow assured him Mr Swayne had picked it up and it was quite safe. After that he really did go mute. I suppose it was catching up with him by then."

Perhaps. But for some reason it failed to sound like Bossie.

"Any use my putting a man in with him, in case he wakes up and wants to get it off his chest in the night?"

"Wouldn't get you a thing," she assured him. "He's as good as out now, and he'll sleep right through until tomorrow. You can make it fairly early, though, and see if he's awake about seven.

So that was that, and the arrival of Sam and Jenny, roused and anxious but calm, brought the number of people attendant upon Bossie to an inconvenient crowd.

"Come on," said Willie the Twig practically, "they're not closed yet, and I'm hungry. And I rather think the Superintendent would like the first-hand story from us, at any rate, since he can't get it yet from the kid. Let's all go and get a pint and a snack at the 'Fleece', and

George can ask us whatever he wants to know."

They left both cars where they were, safe in the hospital grounds, and walked the few hundred yards to the 'Fleece', an old, half-timbered pub, with mediaeval tiles still paving its short passage to the public bar. There were deep settles in which small groups could be as private as in separate rooms, and if the bread, though pleasantly crusty, was slightly past its best at this time on Saturday night, the cheese was good, the ham even better, and the pickles home-made.

"It was going to be a slap-up dinner over at the 'Radnorshire Arms'," said Barbara, buttering bread with ardour. "But that went for a Burton. Tomorrow, maybe?" She looked across the table at Willie the Twig, and her eyes were large and eloquent.

"If we're still out of jug," said Willie imperturbably.

"Maybe George could arrange for a double cell," she said serenely. "That would be nice."

"If you're trying to tell me something," said George tolerantly, "I'd rather you did it right-way-round. But first of all, about tonight. Let's have your version."

"We were going out to dinner," said Barbara, "as we've mentioned, and then we were going to have a lone night drive round through Wales and come back over the border to the forest lodge. Time was no object, and I was driving, and I'm wary of those dark, winding, narrow farm roads, in any case, so we were only doing about thirty, probably less. We hadn't seen another car since we turned into that road, and you know how it winds. One thing I'll swear to, there weren't any car lights on, anywhere ahead of us. Even with those hedges cutting off direct vision, in that darkness there'd have been a gleam, enough to see. Agreed, Willie?"

"Absolutely. And then suddenly there were lights, just switched on, obviously, some way ahead and round a couple of bends, but you see the aura clearly enough."

"And it stayed like that maybe half a minute," confirmed Barbara, "by which time we were getting nearer," and then suddenly whoever it was opened the throttle and put his foot down hard, and the light patch shot off like a bullet. By the time we turned into that longer straight, just past the end of the lane, the rear lights were pin-points at the far end, and then vanished. Then Willie spotted the little boy, lying in the road. And we stopped, and went to see how badly he was hurt, but it wasn't so bad after all. And Willie stayed with him and went over him for breaks and so on, and wrapped his coat round him, while I dashed off back to telephone. And that's about all."

"I lifted him to the side," said Willie. "I thought I'd better, and there was nothing busted, it was safe to move him. But I marked the way he'd been lying."

No particular surprise that Willie the Twig should have a stick of chalk somewhere in his pockets. He was the sort of man who habitually had string, nails, screwdrivers, and half a dozen other useful things distributed about his person.

"And the timing?"

"We left Barbara's place just after nine,

say five or ten past. I reckon it would be about five minutes later when we heard the car shoot off like that."

It fitted. And possibly the simple theory that a courting couple had been making use of the Lyons' drive, and taken to the road again without due care, was the correct one. But there were things about the affair that pricked in George's mind like burrs.

"Then this car, apparently, was parked well up that sloping lane absolutely without lights?"

They looked at each other, and confirmed with an assured exchange of glances that this was so.

"No mistake about it. If they'd even had sidelights on I believe the faint radiation would have shown. When the lights came on, the car was out on the road."

So what would even a courting couple have been doing, drawn in on the grass in absolute darkness, to their own peril? What were the odds against any such car sailing carelessly out and knocking down probably the only pedestrian in all the miles of that road at that time, just by chance? Chance is very, very methodical in its distribution of probabilities, and uses sheer coincidences only very sparingly.

"Or, of course," pointed out Barbara obligingly, "you may take the view that this is simply our concocted story, and we first knocked the child down and then picked him up again."

"And drove the other car away by remote control? Of course, you were the one who went to telephone, and then set off with the ambulance. You haven't actually inspected the place where somebody certainly was parked, backed up into the side of the lane ready to drive out on to the road. Maybe Willie did see it before he left. The other car was there, all right, he brought some fragments of grass and fresh hawthorn leaves out with him. By the way, where did you leave the Land-Rover?"

"On the gravel in front of the house," said Willie, surprised. It took him a second or two to get the drift. He grinned. "True, that would leave me without transport, wouldn't it, if we were working our way round to come to my lodge from Wales. Unless, of course, I was coming all the way back to Abbot's Bale with Barbara. By which time it would be rather late to set off back up the valley with the Land-Rover. Nice guessing, and only slightly wrong. Actually, we were planning on spending the night at my place, not hers, and driving down in the morning."

That fitted, too. If they had driven away from Abbot's Bale House openly in the Aston Martin, and left the Land-Rover standing on the forecourt for anyone to see who cared, plainly they had opted for a policy of complete openness. Which, George recollected, had hardly been Barbara's attitude two days ago, so it must be Willie who had made the decision, and convinced her of its rightness.

"Am I allowed to ask you again, Mrs Rainbow," said George equably, "whether you want to alter your amended account of Thursday night? In the light of all this, I feel I'm being invited to show an interest."

"On Thursday night," said Willie firmly, "Barbara left as soon as her husband was off to choir practice, and drove up to my place. Not for the first time. We were there together from about half past eight until half past eleven, when she left for home. By which time, I gather, her husband was dead. Barbara told you a tall story because she didn't want to bring me into the affair at all. Which was nice of her, but pointless, since I am in it, and in any case it means that I can vouch for her absolutely. When somebody killed Rainbow, Barbara was up in the forest with me."

"Idiot," said Barbara, affectionately and serenely, "don't you see that leaves us both in it up to the neck? Obviously, each of us would be ready to give the other an alibi any time of the day or night, but what makes you think George has to accept that?"

"Idiot," said Willie, just as buoyantly, "do you think that makes us any different from all the rest of Middlehope? There isn't a native up there who wouldn't give every other native an alibi, as against the aliens. George knows it. Even if he didn't — but he does! — Jack Moon would have told him. That puts us just alongside all the rest. Even if we happen to be telling the truth! In any case, where else would we want to be?"

It was a point of view which George could appreciate, but one, plainly, which had never fully dawned on Barbara until this moment. She laid down her knife, and gazed wide-eyed at Willie across the table, and her slow, astonished smile of acceptance was something to see. That Willie the Twig should include her without question in that 'we', as though she had been born and bred in the secret world of Middlehope, as he had, charmed and flattered her. That he could do it without in the least considering that she should feel charmed and flattered was even more staggering. Love was one thing, love you couldn't help, it went out to alien creatures if it so chose, and there was nothing you could do about it. But this patient, assured instruction that she belonged, and ought to have the sense to stop behaving as if she did not, this was quite another matter. There were startled tears, as well as irresistible laughter, in Barbara's eyes as she agreed almost meekly:

"That's right! So we're still in the running, along with all the rest of the valley."

"Neck and neck," said Willie the Twig heartily, and speared the largest remaining pickled onion.

★ ★ ★

Bossie awoke when the light of a fine Sunday morning reached his face, and lay blinking at all the whiteness that surrounded him, and wondering where he was. They had put him in a single room so minute that there was no room in it for much beyond the bed, the inevitable bedside locker, and a tiny wash-basin. There was, however, a large and eastward-facing window, which let in the sun into his eyes. Not home, that was definite. So there had to be a reason, and that started his memory working overtime at picking up clues out of what began as a nightmare agglomeration of disconnected impressions. Darkness, and car noises and car lights, and rolling face-down on spiky boulders like a fakir on a bed of nails. And something crazy, a face of

162

extreme beauty leaning down over him, and a voice like a velvet paw stroking his senses — Bossie knew about voices, and this was a show-stopper.

He moved, and a lot of things hurt, but not acutely, just protestingly, to remind him they were there. Especially his left hip and side, on which he was lying. He turned over, which also hurt, and then he found the pillow rasping his right cheek. The safest position seemed to be flat on his back. Like a sensible person he adopted it, and heaved himself up slightly on the pillow, and settled down to think things out.

If his muscles were stiff and sore, there was nothing the matter with his mind, once it came awake enough to function. He remembered walking along the dark road from the bus stop, as he had done dozens of times before, and then the terrifying rush of air and metal and bulk bearing down on him from the lane on the right, in total darkness until the headlights suddenly sprang up to pin him. He remembered the jolting pain hoisting him by the left hip and slamming him down on the road,

163

grazed and stunned, and the indignity of struggling to move, and not being able to shift his weight by an inch. Just like the kind of nightmare where you fall down in front of a steam-roller, and watch it approaching, dead slow, and find your own movements even slower, absolutely helpless to remove you from its path.

He lay thinking with his usual concentrated ferocity, and the longer he thought, the clearer all the details became, things he had never consciously noticed at all. And the clearer the details became, the clearer still did it become that Bossie was in need of help. He could no more tell the whole truth now than a couple of days ago, when he had carefully refrained from telling any of it; but the hour had clearly come to pick his way gingerly through the minefield, and unload at least a part of the burden on somebody official. While he could!

A skittish nurse came to take his temperature, asked archly how we were feeling this morning, and generally behaved as to a juvenile of doubtful intelligence, which was all the more offensive because she was barely six years older than he was. Bossie refrained from blasting her until she had brought him his breakfast, a sensible precaution, and then demanded to know how long he was going to be kept here.

"Once the doctor's seen you," she said goodhumouredly, "they'll probably throw you out. Your folks are coming in later to take you home."

"Then before they come," ordered Bossie firmly, "I want to talk to the police. Somebody sensible. Sergeant Moon would do." For what had happened to him had happened in Sergeant Moon's territory, and he would certainly have been informed of it.

"Now isn't that convenient," said the nurse smugly, "seeing the police are here to talk to you, and the doctor says they can? It isn't Sergeant Moon, though, it's Detective-Superintendent Felse. You must have been up in the top reaches of crime to have the C.I.D. after you."

He didn't resent that; it was, after all, badinage of a kind rather flattering to his ego. He was busy arranging within his mind what he could and could not tell, and stepping delicately round the places

165

where they overlapped, and by the time George came in, closed the door, and sat down beside the bed, Bossie was ready for him.

"How are you feeling?" asked George. "Fit to talk about it?"

"Yes." He had made up his mind to that, but there was still a certain tentative look about him, as though a degree of editing was going on behind his corrective lenses. His right cheek was grazed and swollen, but the damage was not great, and beauty had never been Bossie's long suit. "I was walking home from the bus," he began briskly, for this was only the preface to the real story, "and I was just past the end of the lane from the farm, when all of a sudden this car came rolling down the slope and out on to the road, and turned after me. There hadn't been a sound until then. He never switched on his engine or his lights until he was out, and then he came straight at me. I jumped for the hedge, but the wing hit me and knocked me down, and I was sort of stunned."

"And he stopped when he was past you?" prompted George.

"Yes, a few yards past. I tried to get up, but I couldn't move, and I could see his rear lights right in front of me."

"So it looks, doesn't it, as if he meant to do the right thing, and stop and salvage you, and report the accident, if he hadn't lost his nerve when he heard another car coming? You know, don't you, that Mrs Rainbow's car came along, and she called the ambulance and the police, and came down here with you?"

"No, really? Was that who it was?" Momentarily sidetracked into the recollection of all that indignant beauty bending sympathetically over him, Bossie gaped and dreamed. "You know, I don't remember ever seeing her close to, before, only going past in the car. She didn't come to church, only once or twice." Not surprising, thought George; Rainbow's preoccupation was her respite. "But it wasn't like that," said Bossie returning to the matter in hand. "It wasn't an accident. And he didn't stop because he'd hit me — he stopped because he'd missed me. He stopped to have another go."

After a moment of silence, though not of complete disbelief, George said reasonably: "You'll have to justify that, you know. Go into detail. There must be certain things that have given you that impression. Now you tell me. You were lying half-stunned, but you say you could see his rear-lights only a few feet away. Then you must also have been able to see his number-plate, though you may not be able to recall it now."

"No," said Bossie, with a hint of satisfaction, "I not only don't remember, I never saw his number. There was only a blank between the rear lights. Dull, like sacking. I think he'd got his number-plates covered."

"He'd get picked up if he was seen on populated roads like that." But he was on a road practically deserted at night, and it wouldn't take many minutes to swathe a number-plate, or many minutes to uncover it again, once safely away from the spot. "Go on, you've got something more to say, haven't you?"

"He started backing the car," said Bossie.

George forbore from pointing out the grisly reasons why no sane assassin, having failed in a forward hit, would then back over his victim, but Bossie's next delivery was unnerving evidence that he had thought of them for himself.

"Oh, not straight towards me, over to my left. He started backing *past* me. His front wheels were about by my shoulder when he suddenly changed his mind and shot off at speed and left me there, and I only realised then that there was another car coming along from the village, and he'd heard it and run for it. Before they could come on the scene and get a look at him. If they hadn't come," stated Bossie positively, "he was going to straighten out again behind me — nothing would have shown on the road — and run me over. It would have passed for a hit-and-run, and if he got away all right he'd have plenty of time to clean up the car."

"So what you're asking me to believe," said George neutrally. "is that somebody was actually lying in wait for you there. Expressly for *you*. Well, before we go into that, can you give us anything on the car? Registration, obviously not, but anything about it? Description, colour, size?"

Bossie showed embarrassment for the first time: of all the things this noticing child failed to notice, mechanical objects held the least interest for him, even in broad daylight, and this had happened in the dark. "Middling-sized," he hazarded dubiously, "and dark, but I never really *saw* what it was like. But it had a good sort of sound when it took off — you know, quiet and fierce . . . "

"Hmmm, pity, but let it go. Now, if this was a deliberate attempt on *you* — you are saying that, aren't you?"

"Yes," said Bossie with finality.

"Then how would the person concerned know you'd be passing there at that time?"

"I think," said Bossie carefully, "he followed the bus up from Comerford, or maybe from somewhere in between. There was a car went past just as I was getting off the bus. I did have a sort of feeling I heard the same sound again, ahead, when I was walking home. I'm better at sounds, you see, I notice them more. If that was him, he'd have had time to get into position before I got near the place."

"In which case he'd have to know in advance who you are, where you live, which way you'd be walking."

"I think he does. Even which night I go to music-lesson. It isn't often I'm out in the dark on my own, he'd need to do his homework on that, wouldn't he?"

The surprising child was actually becoming involved in this puzzle, even enthusiastic about it. From the safety of a bed in hospital the terrifying aspects were gratifyingly distant and vague. Sitting snugly here under police protection, he was beginning to feel like the hunter instead of the hunted.

"Right, now tell me one good reason," said George gently, "why anyone in the world should be lying in wait for *you* — specifically *you*! — with murderous intent?"

"Because," said Bossie, taking the plunge, "I was hanging about in the churchyard the night Mr Rainbow was killed, and he's afraid I may be able to identify him."

He was relieved to observe that there was going to be no out-and-out disbelief, no exclaiming, no time wasted in casting doubts on his memory or his veracity. George merely asked at once: "And can you?" Bossie approved that. First things first.

"No, that's the hell of it, I don't know a solitary thing that would pick him out from anybody else. But *he* can't be sure of that, can he? Because I did see him, if you'd call it seeing, when it was among the trees there, and pitch-dark." He gazed rather deprecatingly at George, and said apologetically: "It's a long story. I ought to have told you before, but we were scared. But it was only a leg-pull to start with, we never meant to do any harm."

"Suppose you tell me now? Do you want to wait until your parents come? They'll be in to collect you in an hour or so, you can hang on until then if you like. Or we can have in Sergeant Moon and listen to it now, if that's what you want."

Bossie scorned the idea that he needed his hand held while he trotted out his confession. "They won't mind you and Sergeant Moon," he assured George generously. "I'd rather you heard it first." The protecting arm of the law might be valuable in more directions than one.

"All right, then, that's what we'll do." And George went to summon the sergeant, who came in placidly nursing a notebook, and greeted the patient with a cheerful lack of condescending pity. He had known him from birth.

"A fine how-d'you-do you set up for us last night." he said accusingly, and against all regulations made himself comfortable on the bed. "You can tell the docs aren't worrying about you, or they wouldn't turn us loose on you. All right. I'm set. Get on with it."

Bossie squared himself sturdily back against his pillows, and got on with it.

"It started with an idea I had, when nobody seemed to know what to do to get rid of Mr Rainbow." The infelicity of this opening, luckily, did not strike him. "Nobody liked him, everybody wanted him to up-anchor and go away somewhere else, but nobody was doing anything about it, and the longer he hung on, the harder it was going to be to shift him. So I had this idea. I thought if we trailed some bait for him, some sort of an antique, and made a fool of him in front of everybody, that was the one thing he wouldn't be able to stand. Like these art critics, after they've been had for suckers by fake pictures. Well, I had a thing I thought might do the trick. It was a leaf of real parchment, with bits of at least one lot of writing on it in Latin, only I think it had been cleaned, but not very well — you know, to use again. It was pretty faint, anyhow, but it was really old, and I did it up for him specially. I borrowed one of Dad's books for a copy, and cooked up just a few words in Latin here and here, sort of half faded out, so you could just read a bit about some land with its 'purtenances, and I got in the word 'gold', I knew that would fetch him. And at choir practice I stayed behind and showed this to him, and told him where I'd found it, and asked him what it was all about, and if it was important . . . "

"And where did you find it?" asked George, as Bossie paused for breath. "You told him. You haven't told us."

"In one of those old chests up above the

bell-ringers' room," said Bossie without hesitation. "I was up there with Mr Llewelyn, you know, when he went to take the swarm that got in there."

"Why hadn't you shown it to the vicar, or your father?"

"I never thought much about it, I just kept it as a trophy. I still don't think it's anything much," said Bossie, shrugging it off with disdain, "but I made it look good for him. And he bit like anything. He behaved very offhand, but I knew he was interested. He said he'd take it home and study it properly, and he asked me if I'd shown it to anyone else, and when I said no, he said better not, until we found out whether it was of any importance, but he doubted if it would be. So I knew if it looked good to him he was going to keep it for himself. It didn't really matter, though, whether he went rushing to the vicar to boast of a great find, or hung on to it and never said a word, because either way we could show him up for a fool or a thief, and either way he'd be the laughing-stock of the place. He'd never stand that, he'd pull up his roots and go right away. That's what everybody wanted," said Bossie simply, "but they left it to us to do something about it."

"But for heaven's sake," said George helplessly, "how could you hope to take him in? He can't be an expert on everything, but at least he'd know a genuine membrane of parchment when he saw one — "

"But it *was*, you see! According to Dad's books, the writing on it, what you could make out, was about thirteenth century. So I made my bits from a copy rather later, to be on top of the old one. It looked pretty good. Anyhow, he took it fast enough, didn't he?"

"Quite! He wouldn't pass up the chance, however small, I suppose. But it wouldn't take him long to see through it. Even the modern ink would give you away."

"It wouldn't, you know. Oh, it wasn't proper thirteenth century ink, but it was seventeenth — I got the recipe out of *The Compleat Houfewife*, with walnut-shells and skins and all, and oak-galls. It came up a sort of faded brown. He might think it a bit fishy, but he wouldn't

176

find it was modern, because it wasn't. And I cut a proper quill to do the writing with. And he *was* taken in! He must have been, because the next week at choir practice — That was the night it happened," said Bossie, suddenly stricken at the recollection. "I asked him if it was anything special, and he said no, it turned out to be quite worthless. But he didn't give it back! And after practice he stayed behind, and he'd asked me specially where these chests were. We were all going along home, and I heard the organ playing again, and I knew he was staying behind to have a look up there privately. So I went back. I was wary of going in, so I just waited among the trees, where I could watch the door. I knew I should hear when the organ stopped, and then I was going to creep into the porch and watch what he did. But I gave him a few minutes to come down from the organ, and I was just on my way to the door when somebody came walking out."

"Somebody came out? Mr Rainbow himself?"

"No, it wasn't him. I thought at first

it must be, and after all he was just going home, quite innocently. But I had to duck out of sight myself round a corner, not to be spotted, so I never did get a look at whoever that was. But I realised at once it couldn't be Rainbow, because he didn't stop to lock up, he just walked out of the lych-gate and went away. Then I didn't quite know what to do, but I hung around for a bit, and I was just making up my mind to go home and forget it, when he fell. Crashing down among the grave-stones. I didn't even understand what it was that had fallen, I thought a piece of the parapet must have dropped off. I was even going round that way to have a look, when I heard somebody else coming along between the tombs from the church door. I was among the bushes, a fairish way off, and I lay low there, and saw this sort of dark, stooping shape hurrying along, almost running. But that's all it was, just a shape. Then he stooped, and stooped down lower, and switched on a flash-light, and his other hand was just turning up something to look at it in the light. I knew the way it moved it wasn't stone, and then I saw it was Mr Rainbow's face. He was dead," said Bossie, flat-voiced and huge-eyed, "I knew he was dead. He couldn't have been anything else."

"What about this chap standing over him?" demanded Sergeant Moon briskly. deflecting the fixed gaze to a more bearable target. Bossie blinked and shook himself, and ceased to stare.

"It was very dark, and the torch went out very quickly, and made it seem even darker. I just don't know! I've been trying and trying to think of anything special about him, but I couldn't even tell whether he was tall or short, he was stooping and running. I'm sure it was a man, but that's all I'm sure of. Honestly, if he thinks I could recognise him again, he's crazy. But he'd be even crazier to take the risk, wouldn't he?"

"Assuming he knew you were there at all, yes," agreed George cautiously. "But up to now there's no reason to suppose that he did."

"Oh, yes, he knew. I was in the bushes, and I must have made some movement that made them rustle, because this man suddenly straightened up and seemed to be staring right at me, and I just turned and ran for it, and I knew he was coming after me, and then after all he stopped, and I just went like a bat out of hell for home."

"There you are, then," said Moon with monumental calm. "He may know there was *somebody* there watching, but he still doesn't know who."

"Oh, yes," said Bossie, with a superiority at once smug and desperate, "he does. It wasn't till I got home I found I'd lost my copy of the anthem we'd been practising. It was Locke — 'Turn Thy Face from my sins,' — "

"Very appropriate," murmured Moon, but Bossie was not to be soothed or diverted.

"I had it folded and stuck in my blazer pocket, you see, and it was too long, and stuck out rather a way, and it must have fallen out while I was running. I looked for it the next day, after you'd all finished and gone away, but I never found it, and I bet you didn't, either. Because I reckon he found it first. It had my name and address on it," said Bossie, between terror and triumph. "That's why he was waiting to come at me out of the farm lane, last night."

6

"WELL," said George later, when Bossie had been handed over to his parents, and they were comparing notes in sober retirement, "true or false? You're the expert, you know Bossie better than I do. How much of that story are we to take absolutely seriously?"

"All of it," said Moon. "We can't afford not to. He isn't a liar, he's never had to be, not having had the slightest reason to be scared of telling all to his folks. But there are one or two things that bother me. I'd say it was the truth, but not necessarily nothing but the truth, and probably not the whole truth. Anyhow, Sam confirms that Bossie asked about early scripts, and borrowed a book from him, and was shut up with it over a couple of evenings, concocting this fake of his. He'll have to come clean to his parents now, maybe they'll get more out of him."

"He certainly had a genuine leaf of parchment, or Rainbow would never have been hooked. He told Rainbow he'd found it among the junk in the tower, and Rainbow shrugged it off as junk like the rest, but he didn't give it back, and he discouraged further interest in it. It really looks as if he may have intended — even begun — searching through the rest of the stuff up there. Hunting for more of the same?"

Sergeant Moon shook his head dubiously. "Even if manuscripts weren't his forte, he could hardly be taken in by Bossie's little effort. I don't believe it for a moment — even if it were a marvel in its way."

"Neither do I, Jack. But don't forget this was a genuine leaf, with the incompletely erased traces of previous use on it. Maybe Rainbow saw through Bossie's palimpsest in more ways than one, and saw something he thought might turn out to be very valuable indeed. Because it looks as if he went hunting where he was told this leaf had been found. What did he think he'd got hold of? One membrane of some church accounts? A leaf of a chronicle? A poem or a lampoon of the time? That sort of thing could send an antiquarian up the wall, let alone up the tower. It might even get him killed, if somebody else with the same acquisitive instincts nosed in on the scent."

Sergeant Moon eyed him steadily in silence for some minutes, and thought about it. "It fits. But we're back to the point that was sticking in my gullet. Bossie says he found that among the oddments in that chest. If what you've just suggested is anywhere near the truth, and that thing we've never set eyes on was a real find from centuries back, then Bossie never found it where he said he did. We've been through all that lot, interesting enough, but not a thing there goes back beyond seventeen-seventy, and most of 'em are Victorian. Why should one leaf survive there on its own? And how could the Victorians miss it, when they made the place over and dumped their own contemporary magazines? No, not a chance. That isn't where he got it."

"Then where did he get it? And above

all, why won't he *tell* us where he got it?"

He had told them, George was sure, everything else. He might recall a few more details, or points that had escaped his first account, but basically he had come clean. So why this one evasion, when evidently his intent was to be as helpful as he could? Who had better reason? Another child might have accepted what happened to him as a real accident, and emerged merely shaken by the chance hurt, and more cautious thereafter. Bossie had come out of sedation wide-awake to the full implications, decided on confession, and almost certainly taken it to the limit. With this one reservation! Why?

"At least he'll be in bed for today, and home and watched even tomorrow," said Moon. "And Sam knows the score now, and we can lend a man now and then, short-handed as we may be, if there should be any need. As long as he's going to and from school by bus with the whole gang, he's as safe as houses. Joe Llewelyn will make sure he's seen home from next week's choir practice.

185

We'll manage to keep an eye on him, between us. And I take it there won't be any headlines from this incident, not unless or until we've got our man. Just a random hit-and-run."

"That's all it will be. I'll see to that." So the would-be assassin would be left in the dark, assuming, it was to be hoped, that the child had neither dreamed of deliberate harm nor blurted out any reason for it. From which he might, with luck, deduce that his fears were baseless, and this intruding imp had nothing whatever to tell about him.

Even so, Bossie knew very well that everybody would be conspiring to keep a more or less constant watch on his welfare from now on. The most staggering thing about the whole interview had been his flourish at the end, when he knew his parents were outside the door, and was graciously saying goodbye to his police guard. He had been wide awake and sparking on all cylinders then, stimulated to such an extent that he was riding high above the danger of which he was, none the less, well aware. After all, it was his act that had set off this explosion wasn't it? And his person that was at risk as a result!

"I say, Mr Felse," he had piped after them, when they were halfway to the door, "what's it worth if I let you use me as bait?"

George had replied without excitement, and without more than a casual turn of his head: "A thick ear, I should think, if your dad ever hears about it." And had departed, secure in his knowledge of the solidity of the family relationship involved, to relay the facts to Sam and Jenny, and assure them of his support whenever they might feel the need of it.

All the same, Bossie was a force to be reckoned with, like all unguided missiles, and George was not going to be the one to underestimate him, or take his quiescence for granted. And the sooner this case was wound up with the murderer in custody, the better for the peace of mind of the Jarvis household.

"Hang on to everything here," said George, making up his mind, "and I'll be back. I'm going to see Mrs Rainbow."

It was Sunday morning. The bells of St Eata's were pealing for the eleven o'clock service, and Spuggy Price would be standing in for the star treble. Only three mornings ago, Arthur Everard Rainbow had been alive and intent, planning his evening's activities at and after choir practice. And what had seemed worth pursuing to him then was worth pursuing now in fairness to his shade. Arid and unregretted, that ghost cried for consideration and redress. George turned in at the lion-guarded gates, and threaded the nymph-haunted drive.

He had wondered for a moment if the Land-Rover would still be parked on the gravel in front of the house, but then dismissed the idea, even before he emerged from the screening trees to see that the lunette of gold was empty. Openness might be the order of the day, but somehow he was certain that Barbara and Willie would find it uncongenial and unsuitable to be together here in this house. Up at the lodge, that was another matter. His next thought was that he might have to go there now to find her, but no, she was at home, she opened the door to his ring, and stepped back to welcome him in with evident pleasure.

"How's the Jarvis boy?" she demanded at once.

"Flourishing, I'm glad to say. His parents have taken him home. Give him a couple of days and he'll be fit as a flea. Thanks to you!"

"No word yet on the hit-and-run car?"

"We've got a general call out for it, but there's probably no noticeable damage, and Bossie could give no clear account of it, naturally enough. But there's something you may be able to help me with."

"If I can," she said at once, and led the way into her small sitting-room. She was wearing slacks and a loose Chinese blouse, no trace today of the splendour she had thought appropriate for dinner in public with Willie the Twig. It was as if she saw the thought pass through George's mind, for she smiled rather wryly, and said simply: "The first time I met him he said to me: 'I don't work my way round, I go straight across!' That's good enough for me, too. If I had cloth of gold, I'd wear it for him. George — may I go on calling you George? — I'm sorry Arthur's dead, I didn't dislike him, and he was never unfair to me. But what we had was a business arrangement, understood if never stated. And my fidelity was not among the things he was buying. Not that I've handed it out freely up to now, but it's mine to give. It was!" she amended, and glowed briefly. "Just to put you in the picture!"

"I begin to think you're psychic," George admitted.

"No, just sharp. I've had to be. I don't mind being misunderstood by outsiders, but I like to get things straight with friends. Without prejudice to your job! You run me in whenever you think it justified. Go ahead, tell me how I can be useful." And this time she brought a drink for him without even asking, Scotch and water, to prove the quality of her memory.

"We've learned." said George, "that a week before his death your husband got hold of a document purporting to be a leaf of parchment dating back to around the thirteenth century. Our information indicates that this was a genuine membrane, but deliberately faked up with some new traces of script

190

to indicate re-use after cleaning. Now how capable would he have been of interpreting and valuing a thing like that? How scholarly was he? He knew Latin, for instance?"

Barbara's eyebrows had soared into her hair. "Well, he'd *done* Latin, as you might say. I wouldn't put it much above O level, though."

"This was a thing in which, I imagine, the surface fraud wouldn't be hard to spot. At least to suspect. But what was underneath may have been quite another matter. He'd want to be sure before he either pursued or discarded it. For instance again, was he competent in unextended mediaeval Latin? They used a baffling sort of shorthand. Would he be able to fill out a code like that?"

"No," said Barbara without hesitation. "He'd be interested, all right, he knew things like that could be pure gold, but what he really knew his way about in was pictures, china and furniture. You can't be expert in everything. What matters is to know just where to go for the expertise in the lines that aren't specifically yours. If he had got hold of something like that, he'd need help to assess it."

"And he'd take that risk? Consult someone else who might be fired with ambition at sight of the thing."

"He'd have to, wouldn't he? It would be a far worse risk, from his point of view, to stake on it without being sure he was on to something good. He couldn't risk being made to look a fool. You only have to lose your credibility once in his business."

"Can you suggest to whom he might go for an opinion?"

"I can suggest to whom he wouldn't," said Barbara with conviction. "Not to anyone in his own line. Not within the trade. Two reasons. Those would be the last people he'd risk exposing himself to, in case he was making a fool of himself. And those would be the first people he'd suspect of having designs on his find if it did turn out to be priceless."

"Who, then? A benevolent scholar, who'd look upon such a thing as an interesting study rather than potential money?"

"I would say so. Helpful acquaintances like, say, Mr Jarvis, would never think of making capital out of a professional's confidences." The thought made her look again at the possibility, and see more in it than immediately met the eye. "You don't think he really did go to Mr Jarvis?" She was thinking of Bossie, but of course she didn't know that the membrane had come from Bossie in the first place. "You don't think there could be any connection, surely, with what happened to that child? This is all getting a bit sinister and suggestive, isn't it?"

"No," said George, "he didn't go to Sam. We know that." Interesting, though, to think he might have done just that, Sam being the last person on earth to suspect of coveting somebody else's discovery or taking advantage of somebody else's request for help. "But thanks for the advice, I think you've put me on the right lines."

For with Sam already eliminated, the supply of first-class classical scholars ready to hand in Middlehope, ruling out, possibly, the vicar, who would certainly not have been consulted in the circumstances, was narrowed down to one.

Professor Emeritus Evan Joyce lived in a rambling stone cottage a little way up the valley, with half an acre of garden, a few old fruit trees, about seven thousand books which lined the walls of all the rooms, and a handsome old desk of enormous proportions, situated in a large window and admirable for spreading out several files of notes, translations and authorities, without actually adding a line to the manuscript about the Goliard poets. The visual effect was impressive, the actual business of rambling among these fascinating properties was ravishing, and the fact that every line he pursued was a digression only added to its charm. He had lived with the fully-realised vision of his magnum opus so long that there was absolutely no prospect of his ever producing it in the flesh. There was no need, it already existed, complete and perfect in his mind.

"Why, yes," he said readily, when George put the question to him, "he did come to consult me, in confidence. But that was the week before he got killed, on the Saturday evening. He brought a leaf of parchment, as you say, and wanted my views on whether it was of any importance. Somebody'd been monkeying with it, on the face of it it was a simple fake, but I think he knew that, even if he didn't say so. But the original cleaning had been very cursory, and there was another script below. It looked highly promising. I thought the text could be recovered more or less complete, given a little effort and patience, and I suggested he should leave it with me and give me time to try and work it out."

"He didn't, by any chance?" asked George wistfully, but without much hope. That leaf of parchment was beginning to beckon like the missing link, the key to everything that had happened and was about to happen.

"He did not! The suggestion made him jump, all right, but back, not forward. I must have looked a good deal too interested, and too eager, he changed his mind about trusting me. And from what you say, I suppose I'd told him what he wanted to know. I'd made it plain there was something genuinely promising there. He practically snatched it back, and thanked me, and said he'd like to try it himself first. I tried to get him to tell me where he'd found it, but he turned deaf, and I never did get to know. You haven't found the membrane among his effects, then, I'm afraid? If you have, I wish you'd let me have a few days to work on it."

For all his gentle person and distracted ways, there was a hungry gleam in his eye at the thought, a spark of real and possibly lawless passion. Unworldly scholars, as well as sharp antique-dealers, may develop unscrupulous lusts after such treasure as mediaeval manuscripts.

"No such luck, it seems to have vanished. But thanks for filling in one gap. You didn't think of volunteering the information as soon as the news of his death went round?"

By this time they were sauntering down the garden path to the gate together, and Evan Joyce turned a sharp glance along his shoulder at the question. "Why, you don't think there could be any significance in this, do you? It never occurred to me. Nothing further had happened about it, and I never gave it a thought."

Which could well be true, and yet was somehow not entirely convincing.

"No, I suppose you might not." agreed George absently, his eyes on the uneven path before them, paved long ago, and bedded down into irregular hollows. Evan Joyce trod it lightly and surely. Small feet he had, encased in surprisingly capacious shoes, old, loose, trodden down, bulging at the big-toe joint, and showing a pattern of faint cracks in their leather uppers. The shoes of an ageing man who liked his comfort, and cared very little about his appearance, and kept old shoes until they warped past the point of comfort. He had been out here putting in fresh bedding plants round some of the rose-beds when George arrived, the soil was dark and damp where he had watered them in. George halted to admire.

"Some fine roses you've still got."

"Trimming the dead ones off regularly is the secret," said Joyce heartily. "I usually have one or two at Christmas."

"That's a beautiful yellow McGredy. I never seem to get them as perfect as that," said George guilefully. The bush was well into the bed, beyond the moist band of soil, and Evan Joyce was a small man. And innocent! It was a shame to trick him.

"Would you like a buttonhole?" He hopped gaily over his newly bedded border, and planted his left foot firmly in the darkened soil to clip off the rose; and by sheer luck he turned on his right foot to step back to the path, and left a fine, clear imprint behind him. The right size, with the suggestion of the smaller foot inside, the right tread, down at the outer rim of the heel, unevenly weighted, with a distinct crack at the remembered angle across the sole. George stood gazing at it so steadily and with such intent that his companion, who was proffering the rose in silence, could not choose but follow the fixed gaze and contemplate his own left footprint with the same concentration. He was very astute, things did not have to be laboured for him.

"You seem," he said mildly, and with no particular anxiety, "to have seen that before?"

"I ought to apologise," admitted George,

"for getting a rose on false pretences, though it's every bit as fine as I said it was, and I'll accept it gladly if you still feel inclined to part with it. But the fact is, yes, I have seen the print of your left foot before, in this same shoe."

"Hardly ever wears any others," said Evan cheerfully, "and never to walk far. One's feet do take over at my age, and demand their own way. I have a feeling we might as well go back in, and begin again."

"You are not only psychic," said George gratefully. "but remarkably generous. I do hope you're not a murderer?"

"With my physique? I should need firearms, and firearms would frighten me to death before I ever got near firing them. Come on, I'll make some coffee. If my conscience had been clear, in any case, I should have been at church, but Rainbow was haunting me. I grudged him my choir, you know, not to mention the organ. I don't claim the idea of murder is so far out of court. But I dream, I don't do. Everybody around here knows that." He sounded regretful, and possibly he really was.

Inside again, across the immense desk and over mugs of strong black coffee, they eyed each other with mutual respect, almost affection. Two ageing men, thought George, though he was at least fifteen years behind Evan Joyce, and both with feet that give trouble at times, and have imposed their own pattern on living.

"And on staircases," said Evan, "I do tend to tread well to the outside, spreading the load and the balance. Maybe that was why you got such a good impression. If you want to borrow my left shoe, please do return it as soon as possible, it takes me years now to break a pair in. I can't think why a sedentary worker should put such a strain on his hooves, but there it is."

"I don't think we need deprive you at all," said George, "provided you tell me what your shoe was doing up the church tower on Thursday night."

"I'll tell you the whole thing," agreed Evan sunnily, sipping his coffee. "I can't think why I didn't do it right away, because I can hardly have been afraid to. It may have been local solidarity.

You understand about that. Or it may, regrettably, have been pure laziness. I'm a martyr to laziness."

"That," said George ruefully, "is a kind of martyrdom I should like to enjoy."

"It's the luxury of retirement. Not for you, not for years yet. Laziness without boredom, the delight of being furiously busy doing nothing. Well, you want to know when and how I came to be in the tower, leaving footprints around. It was the night he was killed, of course, though I didn't know anything about that until yesterday, believe it or not. Rumour washes my way, all right, but it doesn't rush, it waits until I crop up, and I don't believe I was out of the garden, or had a letter or any sort of contact on Friday at all."

"Go on," said George, avoiding comment.

"Well, it's simply that I was dead curious about that membrane, and I wanted to find out where he'd run across it, I dare say I even suspected it might not have been honestly come by, when he was so cagey about it. Anyhow,

I reasoned that if it was local it must have come from some source to which he had constant access, and the church was first candidate. So last Thursday I slipped in during choir practice and sat out the session at the back, out of sight. Sundays there are too many people in and out all the time, I reasoned Thursday would give him a better chance for probing, he could easily be the last out, he had keys. The odds against one leaf surviving alone, like that, come pretty high, you know, I reckoned he'd be on the hunt for more, and I didn't see why he should have the field to himself. And sure enough, he let all the rest go, even the vicar, and went back to playing the organ for about ten minutes. Not more. Then I knew he was up to something: He came down from the organ and made straight for the tower door. And I gave him a start, and then came out of hiding and followed him."

"And got — how far?"

"As far as the limbo above the bell-ringers' room. Rainbow was already up among the bells. I dare say I should have hesitated, anyhow, but I was just setting foot on the first tread of the next ladder when I heard voices up above — "

"Voices? There were already *two* of them up there?"

"Well, that's a question. One says voices, because people don't normally talk to themselves. Especially on clandestine business. What's certain is that after purposeful silence, suddenly somebody was talking up there above my head. The pitch of the voices was much the same, so I'd say definitely two men, of whom I naturally assumed one was Rainbow."

"But nobody'd gone up there while you were in the church? Until Rainbow, I mean?"

"Nobody. I couldn't have missed seeing him if he had. But I was only there from about a quarter of an hour before they finished practice, somebody could have walked in just as I did, and been lurking there behind the curtain before I came."

"Could you distinguish words? Or even two different intonations?"

"This is where I fear I prove useless to you," said Evan Joyce almost guiltily. "Both male, yes, pretty certainly. But words . . . ! You go there, Superintendent!

Put a couple of your men up there among the bells, and you stand where I was standing, and listen to them talking. Even full-voiced, and what I heard was muted. The effect is eerie. About five different echoes coming in from all directions, and rolling around off the woodwork and the bells, so that all you hear is a curious, muffled murmur, a distant roar, not even describable, let alone distinguishable. No, I couldn't even make the wildest guess at what they were saying, or who the second one was. The only impression I can pin down at all, and that dubiously, is that there was no pleasure and a good deal of annoyance reverberating round up there."

"We'll make a few tests," said George, but without any great hope of achieving better results. "Then what did you do?"

"I quit. You could say I came to my senses. If that was a snooper up there waiting for Rainbow, here was another down here, and I didn't much like the character. Besides, butting into a twosome is a bit too much. I'm a retiring sort of chap by nature, I know my limitations. I packed it in and went home."

Somebody came out from the porch, Bossie had said, not very long after Rainbow stopped playing. Simply walked away out of the lych-gate and went home. That fitted; so did the spot where Evan claimed to have abandoned his climb.

"After all," said Evan reasonably, "I'd more or less found out what I wanted to know. What else could have sent Rainbow scurrying up the tower among all that junk and dust? Whatever he'd got had come from somewhere up there. I thought I knew now where to look. But I let well alone for a day or so, and then the news hit me, and you were in possession. I surrender! That is not at all my league. And you never found the membrane?"

George saw no reason to hedge on that point. "The fond remembrance of it, and that's all. I'm as nose-down on the scent as you."

"Then whoever killed him has got it," said Joyce. His mild elderly voice was sharp and eager, the metaphor of hounds on a trail was no exaggeration. "That was why he died. So who was that up there? Somebody else he consulted as he did me? I doubt it. I'd given him the green light, he knew he wasn't on a total loser. I don't believe he'd have looked for another expert until he'd done every bit of work on it he could do himself, and made a thorough search for any other connecting leaves there might be to be found wherever this one was found. He wouldn't want to share the glory or the profit."

"I don't know about the profit," said George deliberately, "I don't suppose that bothers you at all. But the glory might."

"Oh, it would, George, it would! I'd almost have tossed Rainbow off the tower myself, to get hold of that leaf. Supposing, of course, I could hope to lift a weight half as much again as mine. But I never got the chance. There was somebody there before me, and I went home."

And clearly that was all that George was going to get out of this interview, apart from one very handsome yellow rose, which Evan Joyce bestowed on him at parting, with a forgiving smile. And it could all be the truth, but the ambiguous quality remained. A passion is a passion, whether for old letters for their own scholarly sake, or for money and kudos, or for a woman like Barbara. And that same old shoe might well have ventured higher, even if it couldn't be certainly identified above. Naturally, too, Evan Joyce would fail to identify any voice in such circumstances, unless he could be sure it was not that of a native. He was part of the same landscape. That puts us alongside all the rest, Willie the Twig had said cheerfully, even if we do happen to be telling the truth.

In any case, where else would any of them want to be?

* * *

At evensong that Sunday the trebles of St Eata's were unusually circumspect and serious, too thoughtful even to play noughts and crosses. Spuggy Price sang Bossie's solo as though his heart was not in it. And the only message that passed along the choirstalls during the sermon was a note saying:

'Deliggation to Bossie's after serviss. Voluntears sine here.' Toffee Bill had written it, and spelling was not his strong point.

By the time they foregathered in the furnace room, to the rolling sounds of a Buxtehude prelude played by Miss de la Pole, they had six volunteers, which all agreed was too many to be welcome to Mrs Jarvis at this time of night. In the end, Ginger, Toffee Bill and Jimmy Grocott were deputised to represent all, and report back next day on the school bus.

Jenny was neither surprised nor disconcerted to receive three solemn delegates asking after her son's progress and requesting to see him. She let them in and sent them trooping up to Bossie's bedroom, where the casualty sat enthroned, surrounded by books and puzzles, enjoying his notoriety. He looked in remarkably good shape, but for his grazes and the hint of a black eye, and his parents were comfortably sure by then that his constitution had survived the shock without damage, and there was no reason why he should not get up next day, and return to school in another day or two. Bossie himself was expecting as much; school was no penance to him. And the great thing was, as his parents had agreed privately, to go on living as normally as possible, and avoid giving him the idea that anyone was keeping a close eye on him. Though, of course, they were!

Bossie shoved the accumulation of books into a single pile, and hoisted them to his bedside table to make room for his henchmen on the bed. "I thought you'd be along," he said complacently.

"Things can't very well be left as they are, can they?" said Ginger emphatically. "Because, even if it *was* only Rainbow, murderers ought to be caught. And anyway, if he isn't, he's liable to have another go at knocking you off. Because he did, didn't he?"

"That's what I think," agreed Bossie firmly, "and if you ask me, it's what the police think, too. I'm sure they believed me."

"How much did you tell them?" asked Toffee Bill.

"Everything I could, everything that only drops *us* in the muck — not that anybody seems at all bothered about what we did. But you know I couldn't tell them how I really got that parchment."

"No," they agreed, very gravely and resolutely, "of course you couldn't."

"So we can't leave it to the police," pointed out Ginger reasonably, "because they've only got half a tale. Where do you reckon that thing is now? You think *he*'s got it?"

"Of course he has. Rainbow must have had it on him, he was cagey enough about it, and nobody's found it since. He's got it, all right. And by now he's had time to study it, too."

"But there was nothing on it, not really," objected Jimmy. "Nothing for him to get excited about."

"That's what we thought! But there was, there must have been. Something he could find in that old writing that was on it, even if it was faint. We *knew* where the parchment came from, *he*'s had to find out by studying it, but there must have been some clue there for him to decypher. I bet you anything he's got a fair idea now where to look, to see if there's any more of it to find."

"It must be something pretty marvellous,"

said Toffee Bill, staring round-eyed at treasures in his mind. "I mean, to make him want to steal the paper in the first place, let alone what he did to Rainbow. There could be a clue in it, couldn't there, to some place where they buried the church plate, when those chaps came to dissolve the monasteries. Or perhaps where the prior hid all the money that was left, when he was shoved out on to the roads, so he or somebody else could sneak back and collect it. Only maybe they killed him, and he couldn't come back for it."

"We don't know what it is," said Ginger firmly, "but we do know it must be something important. What matters is, what do we do about it? We can't tip off the police! If it was only us it would be all right, but it isn't only us. And still we can't just do nothing. So what *do* we do?"

"We tackle it ourselves." Bossie squinted ferociously through his corrective lenses, and scrubbed at his grazes, which were beginning to itch. "Even if he's found a clue to the general area where he has to look, it's still a whacking great barracks of a place, unless he knows just where to search he could spend months going over the whole show. But I know exactly where the leaf came from, we can start looking right there. What we've got to do is beat him to the treasure, whatever it is, and then, when we've got something to show, we can hand over to the police, and let them do the rest. We can easily make up a cover story for how we happened to hit on the right spot. It could be just plain luck, we don't have to split on anybody. If we simply say: Just look what we found, and look where we found it — all innocent! — they'd have to accept that."

"All right," said Ginger, unimpressed but willing. "When, and how, and how many of us? You've been thinking it out, now let's hear it."

"It's got to be safety in numbers, or I don't get to go anywhere for a bit," said Bossie, displaying a comprehension of his elders' states of mind which would not have surprised his parents to any great extent. "So look, as soon as I'm back at school we work this together, the whole gang of us . . ."

He leaned forward and sank his voice to a conspiratorial whisper, and all the young heads drew together over the quilted coverlet in profound session.

They were just about clear and agreed when Jenny, almost excessively discreet, tapped at the door before entering, and opened it slowly to give them time to take in the invading vision.

"You've got another visitor, Bossie. Mrs Rainbow's enquiring how you're progressing. I don't suppose you ever had time to thank her for rushing you into hospital. Now's your chance!"

Bossie shot upright against his pillows, rushed a fist rapidly over his fell of hair, and put on his most adult face. It squinted rather more than was now usual with him, out of pure excitement, but happily he was unaware of that. His dignity was monumental. He hardly needed to cast a glance at his henchmen. They all said goodnight submissively, and trooped away downstairs as if in response to an order. And Bossie and Barbara were left alone.

"Hullo!" said Barbara, in the velvet voice he remembered. "Can I sit on the bed?" She was dressed for a Sunday night up in the forest, but Bossie was not to know that the black and gold silk shirt with the tiger's-eye cuff-links, and the matching head-scarf, and the tapered black silk slacks, were for another male, not for him. Barbara's cloth of gold came in all degrees of utility and display. She was particularly beautiful because she was on her way to Willie the Twig, but the largesse was lavished upon everyone along the way. Bossie expanded and matured like a plant in the sun.

"They wouldn't let me do this in the hospital," said Barbara with pleasure, stretching her long legs and crossing her elegant ankles. "I'm glad they let you out of there so quickly, it proves you're doing all right. What about the bruises? That was quite a crash you took."

And this was the exquisite creature who had leaped out of her car to rescue him, called the ambulance, and ridden with him to the hospital. Bossie submerged in the profounds of love, and was exalted into airborne fantasies of self-esteem. He said all the things he'd dreamed of saying to her, that he was fine, that it was thanks to her, that the bruises were nothing. "You saved my life," he said, and was promptly brought up hard against the realisation that he had been instrumental, however inadvertently, in getting her husband killed, for which her coals of fire seemed a truly crushing return.

Barbara, since her conversation with George that morning, had been thinking much the same thing, but thought it desirable to turn the boy's mind away from any such consideration. She cast about for a neutral topic, and remembered that the child was musical. By the time Sam came up, a quarter of an hour later, rather to rescue Barbara than to protect the invalid, they were chatting animatedly about musical boxes, of all things, and Barbara had promised to come again and show him one that played 'The Shepherd on the Rock', quite beautifully. Almost, Bossie's qualms of conscience had been lulled to sleep, almost he had forgotten what he had just been plotting with his fellow-conspirators. Almost, but not quite.

"Dad," said Bossie, after long consideration, when his visitor had departed, "do you think she really liked Mr Rainbow?" He was naïve enough, and had been fortunate enough in his own opportunities of studying a marriage at close quarters, to suppose that husbands and wives must unquestionably like each other. Yet Barbara's manner, while not suggesting any degree of rejoicing at her widowhood, certainly conveyed no suggestion of conventional mourning.

Watch your step! thought Sam, and took his time about answering. "Difficult to say, but I think they got on quite well together. But sometimes people do get married for different sorts of reasons, that seem sound enough at the time, and then find they aren't really suited. That doesn't mean they dislike each other. The fire just burns a bit dull, you might say, instead of nice and brightly. He was a lot older than his wife, for one thing."

"And that's bad?" queried Bossie, reflecting shrewdly how much younger he himself was. "Is it bad the other way round, too?" There had been a time when he'd thought of marrying Miss de la Pole as soon as he was old enough.

"It complicates things, either way. It's something to think hard about, before you take any rash steps."

"Oh, well," said Bossie resignedly, "she probably wouldn't wait, anyhow. And marrying people isn't as fashionable as it used to be. Lots of lovers get along without it. Even married to other people sometimes, like Tristan and Isolde. Just as long as you don't think she's missing him all that much. And I wouldn't say she is, really, would you?"

★ ★ ★

The inquest on Arthur Everard Rainbow duly opened on Monday morning, and was duly adjourned for a week at the request of the police, after evidence of identification and medical evidence had been given. That took care of any immediate leakage of information, anything that might have betrayed to the murderer a suspected connection between his crime and the 'accident' to Bossie. Keep him guessing, and keep an eye on the boy. The populace of

217

Abbot's Bale might be adept at reading between the sparse lines, but they were not talkers, except to trusted neighbours and friends.

The widow attended, austerely dressed in grey, and behaved with gravity and dignity if not with grief. What was more surprising was that she should be escorted by Charles Goddard, large, impressive and protective, though whether his company and attentions were welcome to Barbara was not so clear. Probably he had taken the responsibility upon himself uninvited, George thought, and that in itself was revealing. He was quite a personality in the county, a widower for some years, and not a doubt of it, he was considerably smitten with Arthur Rainbow's relict. Willie Swayne, of course, worked for his living, and understood that Barbara needed no man to hold her hand on this occasion, and wanted none, either.

The whole procedure took only a short time, and the coroner released the body for burial. The undertakers would collect Rainbow and box him decently, and Barbara would never have to see him again.

★ ★ ★

George drove up the manorial drive once again that same afternoon, and climbed the sweeping staircase to the house.

Nobody let him in, this time. The great front door stood open, and the Land-Rover was parked on the gravel at the foot of the steps. When he rang the bell, Barbara's voice called from the hall: "Come in, George! We saw you coming, we're in here!"

She was in an old plaid skirt and a roll-necked sweater, her sleeves rolled up, and Willie the Twig was sitting cross-legged on one of the elegant Georgian couches, watching her fold garments into a large suitcase on the central table. He looked like a primitive prince supremely calm in his right and his authority, and Barbara had imbibed his certainty, and went about her leisurely preparations in placidity and fulfilment. They were graciously pleased to see George, but would have been perfectly content without him.

"I'm glad you came, I was thinking I ought to give you official notice," said Barbara serenely. "I'm moving in with Willie. Regularising the situation. Or irregularising it, maybe? Anyhow. I never did like this house, and who needs so many things for living? It's all right. I can't officially touch anything here yet, I know that, except my own clothes and things. I'm locking the place up and turning the keys over to Arthur's solicitor, and there's a second set you can have, if you're going to need them."

George acknowledged that it might be an idea. "Have you talked to Bowes yet?"

"About the will?" She smiled, detached and untroubled. "He did call me, by way of an off-the-record bulletin, so that I'd have some idea where I stood. But actually I already knew, you see. I will say for Arthur that he was quite open about it. Fair, too! Everything he offered me, explicitly or implicitly, he delivered, and everything I was supposed to do for him I did. No complaints! Yes, I know just what I'm to get, and I know she gets all the rest. I dare say she earned it, just as honestly, in a way, as I did. I shan't keep the house, or anything out of it."

"I came to pick your brains, actually,"

said George, "over filling in the details of just two days. Your husband came home from choir practice on the Thursday evening, one week before his death, with the leaf of parchment I told you about. That we know. We also know that on Saturday evening he took it to Professor Joyce, and was confirmed in thinking that it might turn out to be something very important, even valuable. After that it seems likely he'd keep it under close guard, and I doubt if any outsider would have had a chance of getting near it, or learning anything about it. But during those two days he may have treated it rather more casually. On the face of it, it was a fake, and he'd know that. But he may not have known, until Evan Joyce got excited about it, that there was something genuine and potentially precious under the fake. I'd like to hunt up all those who may have got wind of his find. Some of his professional rivals have been going in and out pretty freely here, I take it."

"They certainly have," agreed Barbara with feeling. "These Little Nells watch one another like hawks, spy on one another on principle. All's fair! And he encouraged them, of course, the risk was also his own opportunity. Part of my function was to bring them here and set them talking — prise information out of them if I could. No doubt they were doing as much for me. It wouldn't take much to alert them, either. If he even looked excited or smug, they'd begin to probe. But those two days . . . let me think! I had a musical party here that Thursday evening, while he was at practice. He sometimes got more that way, by turning me loose on them in his absence, or he thought he did. Now I come to think of it, he did go straight through into the office with his music-case before coming in to join us, and he locked it away, too. I believe I even said something about how possessive he was looking, something about never knowing where treasure might turn up, even at choir practice. Good lord," she said, startled, "even that could have been enough to start a really keen one on the scent! Do you suppose it did?"

"Who was present to hear it?"

"I'm not sure I can remember them all.

Mr Goddard was here, and he brought a Mr and Mrs Simmons who were staying with him, I'd never met them before. They're nothing to do with antiques, though, as far as I know. Then there was that man who conducts for the Amateur Operatic Society, and Tom Clouston and his wife, they run the gallery in Comerbourne. But they're more new and local things, paintings and sculpture and fabrics and pottery. And John Stubbs. I was having difficulty over getting rid of John at the time, though, so that needn't mean much. He hasn't been around since, probably doesn't like the heat. And Colin, of course, he's usually around. That's the lot, I think. It was just a run of the mill party. Arthur joined us after he'd put his case away. He did look smug. But there was nothing said, of course. I wouldn't think there was much given away that night. But you never know. Really you never know!"

"And the next day, Friday?"

"He was home all morning, and I don't think there were any visitors. After lunch he had a date to play golf with Robert Macsen-Martel at Mottisham, to make up a foursome. I think the other two were Charles Goddard and Doctor Theobald, but you could confirm that with the club. I suppose if he was carrying this thing round with him, he might leave it in his locker, but if it was that precious he'd take care to turn the key on it."

"And the rest of Friday?"

"He was home for tea, which doesn't leave him time for many other contacts. And we had guests for dinner. Nothing to do with trade. He was collecting bits of county, you see, and this was a squireish night." She named the guests. They were antiques rather than antique-dealers, and feudal and distant rather than tribal elements from Middlehope. George shrugged them off resignedly.

"And Saturday — Saturday isn't so easy, because he left for Comerbourne after breakfast. The Clouston Gallery had a ceramics show, and he'd promised to look in there, and then he was going to a small exhibition at the Music Hall, Victorian jewellery, I think. He had lunch somewhere there, but I don't know with whom. He was back before tea, and apparently that's the evening he went to see Professor Joyce. Maybe he had an eye open for a possible safe confidant in town, but decided against it, and preferred to go to an academic here."

"So that's about it. Somewhere along the way, I do believe, somebody got involved. All for a scrap of parchment."

"You really think that was why it happened?" Barbara lifted her head and showed him a face more conscious of pain and waste than he was ever likely to see in Isobel Lavery. "Somebody killed him for a manuscript from the Middle Ages?"

"Yes," said George, "that's exactly what I think. There are other possibilities, but none of them explains why that membrane of parchment has vanished. And when and if we find it, I do believe we shall have found your husband's murderer."

7

"FIVE days!" said Bunty thoughtfully, over the breakfast table on Tuesday morning. "Late to bring in the Yard — for which I'm sure you're grateful — but you do seem to be up against a long slog, don't you? After the almost invisible man. Nothing from any of the local garages on cars with one front wing damaged?"

"Any amount of reports," said George, "all of which petered out on examination. Probably hardly any damage at all, if the truth be known, maybe a slight dent, nothing to be noticed, and he had plenty of time to get well away before we even got the call, let alone felt sure it wasn't an accident."

"So you're left with a list of all those dealers in close competition with Rainbow, especially the ones who were frequent visitors up there, plus all the other guests at his house that particular Thursday evening. Plus," she added

226

doubtfully as an after-thought, "Evan Joyce, who just may have let his scholarly passion run away with him at the sight of treasure. Two days to fill in, in detail, for all those. Quite an order! So I suppose," she ended with a sigh, "I can expect you when I see you!"

"Not even then!" said George, and kissed her, and set off to begin a long day of patient leg-work at the Golf Club.

★ ★ ★

At about this same hour Bossie Jarvis, brushed and fed and fit, his school cap at the approved angle, erupted in the doorway of Sam's study and solemnly reported himself off to catch the school bus down to Mottisham. By this time his grazes had faded to a quiet light-brown colour, and ceased to be glaringly noticeable. He was wearing his Sunday choir-boy look, so glossily clean that it was plain no dirt would adhere to him, so neat that the experienced adult, confronted with him, must instantly be haunted by suspicion of such virtue. His bulging school-bag was slung on one shoulder, and his glasses shone urbanely in the morning sun of what promised to be a fine day.

"I'm going now, Dad!" He had the doctor's permission, and the sense to be just a degree more dutiful and amenable than usual, for reassurance to parents whose nonchalance hadn't got him fooled for a moment. "Ginger and Bill are outside, we shall all be together." Don't overdo it! One step too far, and they'd smell a rat.

"Push off, then," said Sam briskly, aware that he, too, was playing a part, and skating over even thinner ice. "Just as long as you all come back together, too." Not much could happen on a school bus full of riotous youths, and in broad daylight. No coddling, they agreed firmly. One, he wouldn't stand for it, and two, he's smug enough already, deploy an army round him and he'll be unbearable.

"Oh, yes, well, we always do. But, Dad, a bunch of our class are staying later this afternoon and going round Mottisham Abbey with a party. All right if I go with them? We're going to do a project on it." Magic word, terror of all parents whose schooldays occurred before projects were invented to take the place of hard graft. "We'll all be coming back together, only on a later bus. Our passes are OK for any of them. I wouldn't want to miss it."

That, at any rate, was a safe line. Of all the schoolboys Sam had ever known, Bossie was the least likely to want to miss what others might think a deadly dull archaeological visit.

"Oh?" said Sam, turning to look at his son more narrowly. "Who's going from here?"

"Ginger, and Bill, and Jimmy, and Spuggy Price — all our bunch."

From the new comprehensive school at Mottisham to the abbey was not ten minutes' walk, and the escort appeared to be more than adequate. "All right," said Sam, "just behave yourselves and keep off the walls. Don't spin it out too late, though, we've got a visitor coming tonight."

At any other time Bossie would instantly have demanded to know who, out of the practical need to adjust his own engagements according to his liking or dislike of the guest. This time he was too intent upon his own single purpose to prolong the interview, once he had got the permission he wanted.

"Right!" he said buoyantly, "I'll see you later, then." And forthwith departed rapidly. Not until much later did it occur to Sam to remember this unusual want of curiosity, and feel uneasy about it.

★ ★ ★

Mottisham Abbey, according to record, had been in a sad state of dilapidation, physically and morally, even before the king's commissioners made an end of it, and for centuries it had passed almost unnoticed among the ancestral houses of England. Only the former abbot's lodging and a few attached buildings remained in full preservation, turned into a private house after the expulsion of the few remaining monks. Even the church had been in such a poor state of repair that it had been pulled down to provide a quarry for the enlargement of the parish church, half a mile away, and for the private purposes of the Macsen-Martel who had acquired the property. Nobody had ever investigated the relics, or suggested that a dig might be rewarding, until the family, sagging under the burden of maintaining the place, offered it to the National Trust with what endowment they could provide to accompany it. The resulting consultations had brought in various experts, and turned up evidence that the ground-plan of the vanished establishment was remarkably complete at and below soil-level, and showed some unusual features well worth investigating further. Gangs of enthusiastic volunteers had been at work under Charles Goddard's guidance ever since, and still were, laying bare with love the intricacies of a Benedictine house in decline. The property would end up administered jointly by the National Trust and the Department of the Environment, and after renovation they would hope to find a tenant for the house.

This brief introductory history Bossie Jarvis expounded to his henchmen, as they stood waiting to be marshalled into a conducted party, just within the entrance gate at the inner end of the drive.

"You mean they're working like this for nothing?" demanded Jimmy Grocott incredulously, eyeing the distant excavations where the kitchens and offices had once been, where half a dozen students were industriously brushing away at half-revealed stonework, or measuring, or fixing mysterious tags into position.

"Of course they are. They *like* it!" Bossie would have liked it, too, though he would have preferred something that would make faster headway than a small brush. "Not those, of course!" he added, nodding towards the overalled men who were erecting a steel scaffolding round the walls of a huge round building half-seen among the trees of the grounds, and crowned with a fine conical roof. "Those are professionals, they'd never let the public do the restoration work."

"What is that thing?" Spuggy Price wanted to know.

"The dove-cote. That's famous. Maybe they'll let us inside there. There's holes in that lantern in the roof for the birds to get in and out, and all inside there'll be nesting holes in the walls, for thousands of birds. They kept them for food."

"Not much meat on a dove," said Toffee Bill disparagingly. Food was his special subject.

The entire site was a hive of activity, both professional and amateur. At this stage the gardens had naturally suffered somewhat, since half the revelations for which the enthusiasts were digging were under rose-beds and shrubberies. A bewildering number of people were moving about purposefully, paying no attention to the mere sightseers. One conducted party had vanished into the house itself about ten minutes previously, presumably those still waiting would be launched on the same round with another guide as soon as the group ahead had progressed far enough to avoid confusion. Meantime, they looked about them curiously at all this incomprehensible activity, and were not particularly impressed.

"I don't see why the National Trust would want it," said Spuggy, always outspoken. "There's nothing much here."

"They're only just finding out what's

here, and they say it's turning out more important than anybody thought." But Bossie was tolerant of those who did not share his thirst for knowledge, and appreciated their loyalty in assisting him regardless. "What does it matter, anyhow? You know what we're here for."

A few stray adults and a family had joined them by this time. A youngish, dark, sombre man who seemed to be in an official capacity here was looking out from the ticket office, to which he had just crossed from the house, and visibly counting them, and equally visibly frowning at the sight of a bunch of schoolboys at an age he did not trust. He eyed them coldly, said something probably derogatory over his shoulder, to the girl in the kiosk, and went away as abruptly as he had come.

"I hope we don't get *him*," said Spuggy, his hackles already rising. "You know what, I've seen that bloke somewhere before. Up our way. He's been hanging round Mrs Rainbow, but I don't think she's keen."

Their guide, however, when he emerged from the house and crossed the sweep of gravel to collect them, turned out to be a very different person, large, blond and friendly, in a polo-necked sweater and charcoal slacks, casual and reassuring. He had sharp, quirky features, and mobile eyebrows that acknowledged juvenile scrutiny with a tilt that was as good as a wink, and a philosophical grin. He had an air of finding his role as guide, though pleasant and even important, slightly funny. That didn't put Spuggy Price off him at all, quite the contrary. Spuggy, though aware of their reason for being there, was also finding this funny, and if his guide felt the same, the whole round might be enlivened.

"All right, let's go!" said the fair young man briskly, and led his sheep off across the gravel to the arched doorway of what had once been the abbot's lodging. Fourteen in his party, nine of them children! Some of his volunteer colleagues would have blenched, he seemed to be stimulated.

The comparative gloom of the house closed over them, the huge, vaulted hall, the panelled drawing-room. The panelling had been scoured free of all accumulated varnishes, and gleamed pale and shimmering in fine oak, and the ceilings were renovated and beautiful. The guide talked just enough, and listened if other people talked, willing and glad to answer questions, even when the questions were silly, and very soon paying particular attention to Bossie's questions, which were not silly.

"You've been doing your homework, haven't you?" he said appreciatively. "Yes, this is where the king, or any other noble guest, would have been entertained. This wasn't one of the greater houses, but even here, in its heyday, the abbot may have had five hundred guests to dinner. If there was a king among them, the whole house would be given over to him. Of course, when it became a private house, however wealthy, those days were over. The rooms you see have almost all been adapted later. But not the hall."

From the house he led them eastward through a wilderness of truncated flower-beds and scoured areas of excavation, towards what was now the stable block, or had been when the Macsen-Martels could still afford horses and carriages, and arrayed them along a slightly bumpy aisle of grass on the outer side of the stable-block's northern wall.

"Now you're standing in what was once the nave of the abbey church. You can see it's completely gone, at least above-ground. Not so much as the base of a pillar. It wasn't one of the greater efforts, but all its stone was used for other purposes after the Dissolution. And you can see, if we're in the nave of the church, that inside there, in the stable enclosure, that same square was once the abbey cloister. It usually adhered to the south wall of the church, and so it did here. We'll look at that from the inner side on the way back, for that's one wall that's practically untouched since the secularisation."

Bossie was gazing with absorbed attention at that rough stone wall, under its roof of yellow-lichened tiles. Spuggy, on the other hand, was staring in the opposite direction, where, in the middle of what had certainly once been the cemetery of the brothers, two pick-ups were unloading more sections of scaffolding, and two folding metal ladders, and a lorry was tipping cement. There was a mixer turning busily in a corner, under what would once have been the north transept, and a thickset elder shovelling in sand. So much more interesting to Spuggy that he almost got left behind when the party moved on, over the site of the altar and through the gardens, to the dove-cote, where there was a pause to allow everybody to duck inside by the low doorway, and gape up at the vast expanse of wooden framework inside, and the tier after tier of nesting-alcoves.

Jimmy Grocott, whose father kept racing-pigeons, stared with glazing eyes, imagining the flock needed to people such a palace. The guide laughed goodhumouredly, and invited him to start counting, but he lost count before he was a third of the way up the walls. Even when Spuggy Price was discovered three tiers up, head and shoulders into one of the nesting-places, he was merely slapped amiably on the behind, and invited to get down before the warden spotted him. He slid down backwards, grinning, scouring the toes of his school shoes raw on the stonework. They had come to the conclusion that they were lucky in their guide. He seemed quite impressed with Bossie, by the way he kept drawing him out and inviting him to display his knowledge.

"Now we're coming to the edge of the grounds, and as you can see, we've uncovered the outline of a whole range of buildings, that actually stretch away beyond the hedge, under the lane and into the village. Probably the outlying barns and stores go halfway under this side of the housing estate. But these four rooms you see laid out here form a sort of hospital block. The monks' infirmary — then that small apartment, which was the misericorde." He caught Bossie's knowing eye, and grinned. "Go on, you tell 'em what the misericorde was."

"It was where the rules were relaxed, so that the monks who were ill could have special food, and eat meat, and all that."

"Quite right! That leaves two more rooms to the block, the kitchen, and their own chapel. Some of them would be too feeble to get as far as the main church. And close by here was a small cloister, handy for them to take the air if they were fit enough. You can see the shape of the square maintained in the arrangement of these flower-beds, though we may have to take those up later, to see what we've got there."

They had turned back now on a more southerly line.

"Here along the north side of the small cloister a passage ran through to the great cloister, and along this passage were the cells of the scriptorium. I'm sure you can tell us what happened there?"

"It was the place where they did their writing." said Bossie.

"It was indeed. The provision here was fairly lavish, though neglected later. Ten cells, with doors on to the passage and windows to the north. And what sort of writing do you see them working at?"

"Well, letters — there'd be a lot of business to conduct. And then they made their own copies of the Gospels and church service books, and decorated them with coloured initials, and gilt, and all that." Bossie was slightly shaken to hear himself drawing so close to the secret purpose of their visit, led on by this friendly chap who could put up even with Spuggy's exploratory excursions into the stonework, and refrain from saying: 'Don't touch!'

"You know, you could volunteer to do guide duty here any time you've got a free afternoon," said the fair young man, laughing. "OK, what else did they write? Not here necessarily, I'm not sure our lot were all that scholarly by the end, but no doubt they had their day earlier. You can't imagine them writing novels, now, can you?"

"Lives of the saints?" suggested Bossie tentatively. He had seldom had this sort of encouragement anywhere but at home. "And they were the historians, weren't they? I mean, nearly all the records from the Middle Ages were written by monks."

"They were indeed! At St Albans, and Abingdon, and Malmesbury, and Evesham, and a dozen others. What should we do without the monastic chronicles? Yes, they had plenty of writing to do. Right, come along, then! Now we're about at the end of that row of ten cells, passing what was once the south transept of the church, and coming to what looks to you, I'm sure, like a perfectly solid eighteenth-century stable-block, renovated from earlier work, but mainly eighteenth-century."

That was exactly what it looked like, a huge, square enclosure of brick walls, under mellow tiled roofs coloured gold and lime with mosses. There was a little turret over the entrance archway, with a drunken weather-cock leaning at an angle of forty-five degrees, and a clock-face that had been inscrutable probably for a century. A wrought-iron gate had been fitted into the archway, but stood open now, during visiting hours, and admitted the party to a spacious cobbled yard, a filigree of fine green grasses, with coach-houses and stalls round three sides, somewhat decrepit now, with doors sagging or missing. On the fourth side, the north, the full length was obviously one great room, with only one door, at the north-eastern corner, and a range of very high, small windows along the rest of it, tack-room, store and hay-lofts all in one.

"You're looking at the actual shape of the great cloister," said their guide, with a companionable hand on Bossie's shoulder as they entered. "The Macsen-Martel who got this place after the Dissolution kept the whole range of the cloister as stables and stores, and long after that the early eighteenth-century one pulled down some of the decaying brickwork and rebuilt in contemporary style. Just one side he let alone, it was still serviceable. That's this north range. Come on, let's have a look inside."

The corner door was new, and fitted with a lock. This bit was precious, and under treatment. They trooped in after their guide, Bossie with eyes mildly crossed in his passionate concentration, and nostrils quivering.

It was rather dim within there, after the bright daylight outside. The inner wall, windowed as they had observed, let in a certain amount of light, enough to show the lofty timbering of the open roof, and the layout of the flooring, which was carefully roped off in the centre to convey visitors round an area of newly-uncovered tiles, thick russet ceramic patterned in lighter reds and yellows, in designs that added up in fours. Bossie knew them for originals from the Middle Ages, and stared entranced. Spuggy, less impressed, shoved a toe under the rope and prodded the nearest corner.

A voice behind them in the doorway rapped loudly and indignantly: "Don't do that!" They all whirled guiltily to stare at the morose and officious young man who had distrusted them on sight at the entrance. He was just entering from the stable-yard, with an overalled workman at his shoulder, and obviously armed with authority. "We're trying to get this entire pavement restored," he said sternly. "If you disturb what's been done you can cause a lot of trouble. Now, please keep outside the ropes, or you'll have to leave this section." And he gave even their guide a glower, but at once went on with his companion to the far end of the long room, and almost vanished in the dimness.

Bossie had paid attention to this interruption with no more than the surface of his mind. He was staring intently at the rugged surface of the north wall, windowless, jagged, of big, hewn stone blocks. The guardian ropes allowed access to this wall, indeed invited its inspection. It was massive but irregular, probably due for careful restoration, since it was obviously extremely old. The touchy warden and his foreman were conferring over it in the far corner, pointing out certain places to each other, where the stone had weathered badly, for at least three different types of stone appeared to have been used, so that some blocks were hollowed and worn into dimples, while some had shaved off into thin slivers at the corners. It had taken centuries to do it, but time was gradually winning if the game was to bring the wall down. Officialdom had stepped in just in time to save it.

"You know where we are now?" asked the guide.

They knew. They were on the other side of the wall he had pointed out to them at the beginning of their tour of the grounds. Beyond it lay what had once been the nave of the church. They were in the north walk of the great cloister.

"This is the walk that was given over

to study. Along the inner side it was glazed in for shelter, and all along it, where the brick wall is now, there were little secluded alcoves with desks, where the monks could sit and read. Come on, don't let me down, tell us what they were called."

"Carrels," said Bossie, responding almost automatically. His gaze remained fixed on the stone wall, studying the ground along its base, beaten earth cut down to the gravel, all very neat and freshly cleaned. If the tiling extended to this point, it was still buried.

"Full marks! Carrels they were. And on the other side, the church side, that is, along this stone wall, were the aumbries, big cupboards where the manuscripts were kept. I doubt if ours were very elaborate, but beautiful examples do exist, carved and decorated with beaten metalwork. This is the only wall left intact from the very earliest foundation here at Mottisham, that's why it's so precious."

"It's been knocked about since, then," observed Ginger critically. His father was an excellent small builder. "Look at all this loose fill-in rubble stuck into it where it's getting worn. They should have done something better than that to keep it in repair. Look how it's crumbling. And you can see daylight through it in several places. Wouldn't take much to start that piece there, look, it's got a bulge already."

It was true enough. The light inside there was dim enough to let the day glance in clearly in several minute interstices, and the section of wall had indeed a distinct bulge.

"That," said the guide cheerfully, "is exactly why we're taking steps to put it back into condition, but it has to be done with due regard to the old materials, you know. Couldn't knock a section out and fill it in with modern brick, now, could we?"

"You're going to have a big hole here any minute," pointed out Spuggy Price helpfully, and prodded with an exploring finger where a long, narrow, crumbling wedge of mortar was sagging from its place. Proof positive of his rightness, the slice promptly fell out with a clatter, and the warden whirled from his colloquy with the working foreman just in time to detect the crime. Whether he was in a bad temper that day for some quite extraneous reason, or whether he really felt as strongly as this about his charge, he came surging out of his corner in a rage.

"That's enough! Now get these kids out of here, before they bring the whole place down. I knew we were going to have trouble, the moment I set eyes on them. No teacher with them, of course! Pure vandalism! If it rested with me the abbey would be closed to school parties. You, keep your hands to yourself from now on, and please leave this section at once."

"Sorry!" sighed their guide, not greatly troubled but willing to be conciliatory. "I should have put a ban on touching at the start. No harm done, actually, all this rubbish will have to come out, once we begin the job. But I grant you we don't want it out just yet. Might bring the roof down over us," he concluded, and met Spuggy's offended gaze with a twinkle in his eye, and got a furtive grin in return.

The warden distributed a black glare

among them, and stalked out with his attendant on his heels, and the boys breathed again, even giggled a little. "I didn't do his precious wall any harm," said Spuggy. "How did I know that piece would fall out if I touched it?"

"Still, you know," pointed out their guide reasonably marshalling them towards the door, "we'd better do what he says. After all, he's the caretaker here, it's his job to preserve what we've got, not connive at knocking it down. You can't blame him for doing his job."

They supposed not; and they left peaceably, all the more circumspectly, in fact, because the warden had gone no further than the open yard. and was clearly waiting to see them safely off the premises.

"Was it a big library they had here?" asked Bossie, as they walked back towards the gate. "Is there any of it left now?"

"Not a thing, as far as I know. By the end, from all accounts, scholarship was very little regarded here, or sanctity, either. This was one of the houses that had degenerated badly before they were dissolved. There were only four or five monks left, and they had no very good reputation. They're even supposed to have robbed travellers who came here, maybe even murdered one or two. The place was badly run down. Closing it was more or less recognising a fact, though of course the family that got the property benefited."

"But there must have been books. I wonder what happened to them?"

"I wonder, too, laddie," agreed the guide whimsically, as he let them out to the drive, "I wonder, too! Maybe they'd sold them long before, maybe they bartered them for wine, maybe they used them for fuel when wood ran short in the winter. There's certainly no record of any remaining at the end to be dissipated or destroyed. I doubt if the last few monks had any Latin between them. Maybe they used the leather to make shoes!"

★ ★ ★

They gathered at the bus shelter in the village, all of them watching Bossie, who had walked this far in unusual silence and deep, grim thought.

"Was that where he found it?" asked Ginger at last.

"Yes. But it's all been cleaned out there. It was silted up with rubble then, soil and stuff, and grass growing. There's nothing there now. Not unless it's still under the floor."

"Maybe they already found it." suggested Toffee Bill.

"No, there'd have been a terrific to-do about it if they had, in the papers, on television, the lot. We should have heard!"

"Well, we can't do any searching while there's parties going round," said Ginger. "Let alone when *he's* about!"

"No," agreed Bossie weightily. "Not any time when there's anybody about there." The statement sounded faintly ominous, and he was staring so hard into his own mind that his eyes crossed and remained crossed. "I've been thinking about that man. You said you'd seen him up at our place. I think I have, too. I think he came with Mr Macsen-Martel the first time, but he's been to Rainbow's house since then. He didn't like us going in there, did he? Maybe he's like that with all kids, but maybe it was because it was *us*. If we've seen him around, he may have seen us, too."

"You don't think," breathed Ginger, open mouthed, "that it's *him*?" And they all drew closer, awed and chilled, their voices sinking to secretive undertones.

"I don't know," said Bossie. "I can't say he is or he isn't. I just have this feeling about him. He could be. He's here right on the spot, isn't he? And he didn't like us showing up at the abbey at all, and he specially didn't like us poking around by that wall, did he? He followed us in, and he took the first chance to order us out, and he talked about barring school parties altogether, though that may have been just cover, it's us he didn't want there." Bossie made up his mind, instantly and irrevocably, as he usually did. "I'm going to get in there after they're closed!"

They were stricken mute, and could only stare and doubt.

"That's the only chance! And it's got to be tonight. If he's installed there, like this, then maybe he knows already where he has to look, he's just playing it easy and taking his time. It's now or never for us, if we're going to get there first. No," he corrected himself heroically, "for *me*. I started this, and anyhow, it's better only one should go."

"But how will you get in?" they protested, shaken, half wishing themselves bold enough to go with him, half thankful that he was bent on going alone, and that it was he who habitually called the tune. "And what about your folks? They'll go up the wall if you don't show up with us."

"No, they won't, because I'll fix that." He had a friend with whom he occasionally stayed overnight here, when the school had evening events arranged; and though he hadn't involved Philip in this adventure, since it belonged exclusively to Abbot's Bale, he knew he could pop in at the Mason home and ask to use the 'phone to call his mother. A telephone box, of course, would be a complete give-away. With luck he might not even have to let Philip into what he wanted to say, or turn him into an accomplice. Let him go on serenely believing that his friend was merely calling to let his mother know he'd be home by a later bus. While she, naturally, accepted the version that Philip's mum had asked him to stay overnight and go with Philip to the birthday party of another class mate, here in Mottisham. With every possible safeguard, of course! Bossie had a rudimentary conscience where his friends were concerned, but it had elastic properties, too. So even if he had to let Philip into his deception, Philip could be terrorised into secrecy, and Philip's mum would be entirely innocent.

"Anybody got a torch on him?" demanded Bossie, getting down to details. "And any lunch left? But I've got some money, I can buy a pie at Gough's. And if you like to stop over one more bus, you can come along and help me find the right place to get inside the fence. It's long enough, there must be half a dozen good places. And we know the layout now."

He rubbed his hands, already in action.

★ ★ ★

254

"But, lamb," protested Jenny mildly, blissfully unaware that she was talking rather to a tiger on the prowl, "you can't just dump yourself on Mrs Mason without notice, like that. Now don't kid me, I know she'd have called me before if she'd had any idea she was going to have to find you a bed."

"But, Mummy," fluted the distant voice of her offspring, "nobody expected me to be back at school today, that's why. But I *was*, and so I *could* go with Philip, do you see? So can I, please? You know I'll be all right here." That was a stab to the heart, signalling his awareness that his parents might well worry on his account, recent events considered.

"Well, I know birthdays don't occur every day, and can't be shifted, but . . . "

"Ask Dad, though," entreated Bossie.

"Dad is off scouring the library for a reference he couldn't find, you devil. It's me you're putting on the spot. And listen, you don't know the whole of it! We're expecting Toby tonight! He rang through early this morning from Comerbourne, they've got a three-day theatre stand there. You surely want to see Toby, don't you?"

Dead silence and dismay on the line for a moment. Then the voice, very much chastened: "Oh, Mum, you know I do! But if he's got three days . . . Look, you've got to tell him to come again. And we could go and see what they're planning, couldn't we? They want customers! I'd love that, I really would."

Bossie was really aggrieved. Fate ought not to do such unkind things to him. His idol would arrive only to find himself deserted by his most faithful admirer. But he stuck to his guns. "Still, I would like to stay tonight. If I can?"

"If Mrs Mason can put up with you, why should I complain?" At least she knew he'd be under safe-conduct with the Masons. "All right, stay, and mind you make time to do your homework. And telephone tomorrow, to let us know you're OK and on your way to school, you hear me?"

He heard. He said: "Yes, Mum!" with unaccustomed docility, and rang off rather abruptly.

How he was going to get out of this,

in the end, he didn't know, but now he knew past any doubt that he was in it, up to the neck.

★ ★ ★

"I don't like it!" said Ginger rebelliously at the last moment. "We ought to go with you, at least some of us. It isn't right!"

"Don't be daft! One can get by, but if there was a crowd of us we'd be sure to get caught."

"We could hang around here, though, within call. If you were in trouble, you'd only have to yell."

"I'm not going to be in trouble, and I don't want you hanging about, you'd attract attention, lurking about here in a quiet back lane like this. What you've got to do is get on the bus and go home, and keep everything looking normal, otherwise it's all wasted. If I'm lucky, and find something out in time to nip out again before night, I will, and I'll go straight home and tell them. I'm not looking for trouble, all I want is a chance to go over the ground without anyone else knowing, and then it's up to the police. Now I'm going. And you'd better push off, too."

And in the end, unhappily and reluctantly, they did as they were instructed. They were so used to thinking of him as the brains of the outfit that they feared to make any alteration to his planning, in case they wrecked the show. Ginger looked back from the bend in the lane. The loose pale in the tall manorial fence was back in position, there was no rustling or movement among the bushes of the shrubbery within. Bossie had vanished, with his pocket torch, borrowed from Philip Mason under fearful oaths of secrecy, his collection of leftover sandwiches, one apple, and a pork pie from Gough's, in case he really had to stay out all night. Ginger shook his head forebodingly, and all the way home on the bus he said never a word, and even Spuggy Price caught the habit of silence, and stared glumly out of the window.

8

"NO," sighed George, in response to Bunty's unasked questions. "Not a step further forward than we were this morning. Several more reports of dented wings, none of 'em relevant. Rainbow played golf with his foursome, sure enough, and locked a briefcase firmly away while he did it, but as far as we can discover, no one even remotely connected with him was playing at the same time, even if they could have got at his case, which they couldn't without grave risk, because the traffic in and out was brisk, and you don't play tricks with lockers unless you're fairly sure of being undisturbed. At the gallery on Saturday he was among the local artists, who aren't really his cup of tea, and at the Music Hall show all the trade was present, and he might have let something drop to somebody, but if so, none of those we've interviewed got a whiff of it."

"So it's as open as ever," said Bunty, dishing up in the kitchen. "It's what we could have expected. He wasn't a man who generated passions about him. Something quite cold, like greed, knocked Rainbow off. Greed trips over itself sooner or later, or trips over something else quite harmless and incidental. Like Bossie, for instance?"

"As a matter of fact," owned George, relaxing into a tired man's enjoyment of his dinner, after a long day of having no time to be hungry, "I was thinking of going up and having another session with Bossie, now he's home and easy, and his exploits are out in the open. He's had time now to let things relax, and let's hope they've relaxed into focus, not out. There just may be something more he can tell us."

"That reminds me," said Bunty abstractedly. "Thespis is back in town! You remember Toby Malcolm's travelling theatre? They've got a three-day stand from tomorrow, in the Grammar School grounds. They were just getting that odd contraption of theirs fitted up when I came by before tea."

"Really?" Mention of this one glowing success always cheered George, who had seen a lot of failures in his time. "I might just drop in and have a natter with Toby on the way. He cuts a lot of ice with Bossie. Senior and junior partners in crime once upon a time — it has to count for something when the big boy turns legitimate."

In the grounds of Comerbourne's oldest and most illustrious school, still obstinately referred to as the Grammar School though it was well advanced in the process of going comprehensive, there was ample room for Toby's 'three wagons that put together into a rather ramshackle sort of enclosure', and when George arrived there in the dusk the assembly was already complete. October is too late for outdoor theatre in the evenings, and the season of little festivals is over. Presumably schools would have to provide the bulk of support for the rest of the viable travelling year, until Thespis holed up for the winter in some small, friendly town, where at least a few shows could hope for support around Christmas. The seven people, four young men and three girls, who ran the enterprise were shuttling between their odd little theatre and their living van with mute, daemonic purpose, doing mysterious things, and carrying about with them items of costume and equipment even more mysterious. They looked rapt and happy, as people do who are doing, at no matter what material cost to themselves, exactly what they want to do.

Toby came out from the door of the auditorium, which incorporated a ticket-office more restricted than any sentry-box, and saw George crossing from the car-park. He came to meet him at a joyful trot, a coil of cable in one hand and a cassette deck in the other, his thick brown hair bouncing over one blue eye, and a broad, benevolent smile spreading from ear to ear.

"Mr Felse — hullo! Are you after a play-bill? I'm sure Mrs Felse would show one for us, I nearly gave her one this afternoon. But I was stuck like the Colossus of Rhodes at the time, trying to link the third van on. D'you like our set-up? Come and have a look round inside, it's quite safe now. Bounces a bit, but it won't when we've got an audience in."

"Thanks, but I'll wait until we come to the show. Actually I'm thinking of running up to see the Jarvises at Abbot's Bale, and I wondered if you'd be free by this time to come with me."

"No, really?" Toby beamed satisfaction. "You must be reading my mind. I've already promised to go up and stay overnight, now we've got this outfit all set up. I should have been on my way in about ten minutes more. But what with the price of petrol, and all that, I'd just as soon leave the old bike behind, and be driven up there in style. D'you mean it?"

"Of course I mean it. But what about getting back in the morning, if you're staying over?"

"Oh, not to worry about that! I'm sure Sam will drive me down, and drop off Bossie in Mottisham on the way, give the school bus a miss for once. Hang on a couple of minutes, and I'll get rid of this stuff." And Toby turned and galloped enthusiastically to the company's living van and leaped into it like a faun, to reappear in a few moments, hauling on his wind-jacket as he ran.

"I always try to see Sam and Jenny whenever I can. Anyhow, it's home really — apart from that old heap over there, which is home, too, in its way. I'm hawking tickets, by the way, you won't escape. With luck Jenny might plant a few for us up the valley."

"You get me a real lead out of Bossie," promised George, as he started the car and drove out from the school gates, "and I'll buy tickets for every night. You playing in person?"

"Yep! Edgar in *Venus Observed*. Fry's supposed to be old hat, but we always do well with him, and he's such a joy to speak. Edgar 'hangs in abeyance', if you remember. That's usually my fate, partly because I'm the handiest dog's-body we've got behind the scenes."

He would be a charming, slightly ominous Edgar, with infinite potentialities. Very suitable casting, George considered.

"That was our Perpetua you saw trotting across with her arms full of curtains — the one in the tattered jeans. Face like a perverted elf, but she can speak verse like nobody's business. But what did you mean about getting you a lead out of Bossie? *He*'s not in any trouble with the law, is he?" His voice, though light, was also slightly anxious. You never knew what an eccentric genius like Bossie might turn his hand to.

"Certainly not with the law. You probably haven't been following the local press, and in any case it was only a five-line paragraph. Bossie got knocked down by a car — no, don't worry, he's fine, nothing but bruises."

"I didn't know!" said Toby, concerned. "Sam never said a word about it when I called this morning."

"No, well, he'd be leaving it until you could see for yourself there was no damage. You'd have heard all about it tonight. But the thing is, there's a possibility — in fact, we're treating it as a very strong possibility — that his accident was no accident. Bossie happens to have come much too close to this case that's bugging us. You'll have read, at any rate, about Rainbow's murder?"

Toby was gaping at him, aghast. "Well, yes, of course, I've seen all the headlines.

But — You're not seriously saying that somebody tried to run Bossie down with a car? *On purpose?*"

"I'm saying just that. It so happens that Bossie played a certain trick on Rainbow, using a faked antique as bait, and through watching to see what effect his plans were having, he actually saw Rainbow fall, and saw his murderer go to make sure he was dead, and plunder the body. Bossie hasn't been able to identify the murderer, or give us any hint that will help us to finger him. It was a very dark night. Unfortunately," said George grimly, "we have good reason to be sure that the murderer was able to identify Bossie! Hence the attempt on him. We've suppressed any mention of that, naturally, and every care is being taken of him from now on, though it wouldn't do to make that too obvious. What I'm hoping is that now, being further from the event, and in talking to you, not answering police questions, however tactfully phrased, he may pop up with something he doesn't even realise he knows, something that will give us a lead. I'll gladly make myself scarce, if that will help, and leave you to see what you can do with him in the safe surroundings of home. He thinks a lot of you."

"So do I of him," said Toby in a small, shocked voice, and sat and thought about this indigestible revelation for some minutes in silence. "Obviously I'll do anything that may help," he said at last, dazedly. "But how in the world did he get himself into such a jam? Good lord, what does Bossie know about faking antiques? The man was a dealer, and knowledgeable, it would be tough going to fool him, even for a pro. Bossie didn't have anything he could even make halfway presentable for a job like that."

"Apparently he did. He told us all about it quite frankly, except that he said he'd found it among the old magazines and papers in a chest in the church tower. That we doubt. There seems no reason at all why just one leaf should be there, when the rest is nineteenth-century trivia, but he sticks to his story. All he did was doctor it up a little, and clearly it did engage Rainbow's attention — and someone else's, too — not because of Bossie's effort, but in spite of it."

"*Leaf!*" whispered Toby, enlightened and appalled.

"A single leaf of vellum. It bore characters we're led to believe might date back to the thirteenth century. And we're fairly sure it never came from among the old copies of *Pears' Annual* and *Ivy Leaves* up there in the tower. Though why he should tell us everything else, but clam up on where he got it, is more than I can work out."

"Oh, help!" said Toby childishly. in a very small voice indeed. "Now isn't that just like him, the idiot! I'm afraid *I* know where he got it. And why he wouldn't tell you. It's got to be the same one. I know where he got it, because I gave it to him. And I know why he wouldn't tell you that. Because I pinched it, and he knows it, and he probably thinks you'd run me in for it like a shot, even now, if he blew the gaff on me. Bossie would never split on a pal. Oh, now we may really be able to get something more out of him, if he sees it's all come out, and nobody's after my blood. Hell, it was years ago, when I was young and daft."

"Tell me all!" invited George with

268

interest. "This is the first lucky break we've had. This was while you were at school up there?"

"The last year. I never turned down a dare in those days, they only had to throw one at me and I did it, however idiotic. I can't remember who it was, but one of the kids bet me I couldn't break into Mottisham Abbey and get out again without anyone knowing. So of course I did. It was easy, anyhow, I'd broken into far trickier places than that. I brought this bit of parchment out with me just to prove I'd really been there, I didn't consider it was of any value, or that I was pinching anything that mattered. It was a trophy, that's all. I gave it to Bossie as a souvenir, and of course he was sworn to secrecy. Silly kid's stuff, but then, I *was* a silly kid!"

"Well, he certainly kept his oath." George drew hopeful breath. "Who knows, it may be a load off his mind to know it's all out in the open, and nobody's putting handcuffs on you for it. It may even sharpen up his memory to produce a clue for me. So that's where it came from — the abbey! We ought to have thought of that possibility."

"I don't know why. There never was any word said about any records surviving there, the place has always been reckoned a dead loss, without a history."

"Yet this came from there. And it really looks as if Rainbow was killed to get possession of it. Not for itself alone, no doubt — for what further it might lead to. Bossie didn't know his own strength!" They were already through Mottisham, and heading for Abbot's Bale on an almost deserted road. George accelerated purposefully. The sooner they got to Bossie now, and relieved him of the fear of disloyalty to his idol if he talked freely, the sooner they might move on to pursue the real provenance of the membrane that had been the death of Rainbow.

"Do you remember exactly where you picked up this leaf? Was it in the house itself?"

"No. I did get into the house, mind you," owned Toby candidly, "I had to, that was the dare. But I didn't like to take anything from inside there, not even to prove it. No, this was in the stables, in the rubble and weeds under the one wall. I took it for granted it was rubbish, lying there among old junk of planks and mortar, and yet it was something special. I thought it would do nicely."

It had done nicely for Rainbow, and brought Bossie Jarvis into considerable danger.

"Is there really something so important about it? Now you've had time to get it vetted . . . ?"

"We've never even seen it," said George. "We know of it from Bossie, and from one person to whom Rainbow showed it, and that's all. If there's one thing certain, it is that at this moment the murderer has it."

They passed the first cottages of Abbot's Bale, rounded the wall of the churchyard, and turned into the comparative darkness of the lane where Bossie had suffered his adventure. "This," said George, "is just about where he was hit."

"That funny, fool kid!" sighed Toby thankfully. "Praise the lord, you've got a thumb firmly on him now, he can't get himself into any more trouble."

At about this time Bossie was just threading a wary way through the shrubberies, where he had been holed up comfortably enough in a derelict shed with his provender, and had eaten most of it. The students measuring and brushing and marking had gone on working as long as even a gleam of light remained, but they were all gone now, and the whole enclave was silent.

Bossie emerged where the bushes came closest to the brick walls of the stable-block, and allowed him to peer out from cover towards the archway. He remembered the pattern of the gate clearly, and considered that he had two ways of getting to the inner side. One, the bars might very well be wide enough apart to allow him to wriggle through; he was small-boned and agile, and cats can get through wherever their whiskers will pass, as every student knows. Two, the gate did not reach to the summit of the archway, and its surmounting spikes were purely decorative, and could be circumvented with ease. He had no doubt that he could climb it if necessary.

The shadowy bulks of walls and trees loomed immense in the remnant of the light. It appeared to Bossie as still fairly light, for his eyes had grown accustomed to it, having spent some waiting hours adjusting as twilight fell and night came on. But in fact it was a very respectable darkness, as large and awe-inspiring as the silence that was its natural music. There was nothing stirring, not a soul living but himself, and the infinitesimal, furtive night-life of bird and beast. The shrubbery at his back felt like a forest, virgin and strange, but not unfriendly. He was not afraid. When he had stood motionless for some minutes, listening and watching, and was sure he was solitary, he slipped across to the solid reassurance of the wall, worked his way along it to the archway, and slid into the deep embrasure to consider his mode of entry. It was almost disappointingly simple. On the cat principle, he was convinced he could go wherever his head could go, and his head passed between the bars with ease. Sideways, lissom as an eel, Bossie followed his head into the cloister.

It was annoying, after that achievement, to discover that the gate, though meticulously latched, had been unlocked all the time!

★ ★ ★

Willie Swayne's Land-Rover was parked in the drive of Sam Jarvis's cottage, filling the narrow space from clipped hedge to grass-verged rose-bed. The front door of the house was open, and several people were involved in obviously valedictory exchanges just within. George drew up behind the Land-Rover and got out of the car, with Toby hard on his heels.

Barbara Rainbow, with a cotton scarf wreathed round her curls, and her long, elegant body swathed in clinging sweater and black slacks, was talking and laughing in evident familiarity with Jenny Jarvis, as if they had known each other for years. And Jenny was holding before her a small, elaborate casket of polished wood and delicate gilt, and shaking her head deprecatingly over it. Behind them Sam and Willie hovered, complacent.

"He doesn't deserve it," Jenny was saying, turning the musical box about admiringly in her hands, "and you only promised to show it to him, not to give it! I should think better of it now, if I were you."

She had her own ideas as to why Barbara had created this occasion to call on Bossie again, and bring Willie the Twig with her. A pity they'd picked this particular night, and missed him. Bossie was transparent, for all his intellect, and Barbara was a clever woman. Being in love at Bossie's age can be excruciating, but is sometimes surprisingly easily cured. At twelve nobody breaks his heart on the unattainable, and one glance at Willie the Twig in sole possession would have ended that episode. Barbara had even gone to some trouble to ditch all her glamour, though the result happened to be every bit as alluring as when she was in full war-paint.

"There are ten of these things," said Barbara, "and I am not going into business, that's flat. Whoever buys the collection won't miss this one.

And at least we can be sure it'll be appreciated."

That was when Toby appeared, to be greeted with delight and drawn into the group at once, so that Barbara and Willie were deterred from completing their farewells and leaving. George, an ambiguous figure at this hour, when he might or might not be on duty, waited for the social exchanges to come to a natural end.

"Lovely to see you again, Toby," said Jenny, and kissed him heartily. "I hope you're hungry? I know you said you couldn't make it for dinner, but I kept some for you, anyhow. Mrs Rainbow, you remember Toby Malcolm? We brought him with us to your house-warming."

"Of course I remember," said Barbara cordially. "He was the best dancer in the room, we did a real exhibition tango together. And of course you already know Willie Swayne . . . "

"Ever since he clouted me for pinching birds' eggs when I was thirteen," acknowledged Toby, having sized up the situation between these twoL in one shrewd glance. "And then showed

276

me where to watch for otters. Has he taken you there yet? He doesn't show everybody!" One minute flame of male rivalry, mutually understood and enjoyed, subsided again peacefully. Toby couldn't help erecting his plumes for anyone as stunning as Barbara, and Willie, secure in possession, could only be flattered. "Mr Felse gave me a lift up," Toby went on, reverting to business as soon as was decent. "I shall have to cadge a ride back in the morning. He wants to talk to Bossie again." He amended, firmly stressing his own involvement: "We want to talk to Bossie."

"I doubt if you'd get anything more out of him, George," said Sam. "But anyhow, bad luck, he isn't here."

"Not here?" Toby was almost absurdly taken aback. "After a tumble like the one I hear he took, I didn't think he'd be out of the house yet."

"He went back to school today," explained Jenny. "The doctor said he could, he's perfectly fit. And he rang up this afternoon from Audrey Mason's, and said could he stay overnight there and go to a birthday party with her

Philip. Audrey's often had him before, and of course nothing had been said earlier, because they didn't expect him back so soon. He's quite all right with them, you know."

"And he knew I was coming tonight?" demanded Toby, outraged and disbelieving.

"I told him. But he still wanted to stay. I was surprised myself," admitted Jenny.

Toby turned and looked at George, and suddenly and violently shook his head. "I can't believe it. Not just like that!" There's got to be a catch in it. He's up to something!"

"What do you mean? What could he be up to?" But Sam was willing to believe in the possibility of all kinds of complications where his son was concerned. "He intended staying after school in any case," he recalled, frowning. "He told me this morning, a whole bunch of his class were going to tour the abbey — "

"The abbey!" blurted Toby, and gaped at George in wild speculation.

They had all caught the unease by then, and were staring in doubt and misgiving. George said quietly: "I think, Jenny, it would be a good idea to ring Mrs Mason. No point in trying to be diplomatic, time could be important. If he's there, well and good, it's just his mother fussing, wanting to make sure he's all right, and behaving himself. If he isn't, and hasn't . . . well, then it's out in any case. Then I'll take over."

Jenny looked back at him steadily, and steadily turned pale. Without a word she crossed to the telephone and made the call, and all of them watched in intent silence.

"Hullo, Audrey? This is Jenny Jarvis. Can I have a word with our Bossie?" Quite a crisp, practical voice, and then the tight, white look as she listened, and they knew what she was hearing, mild wonder and an immediate disclaimer, and the sharp curiosity not yet expressed. "He isn't there? You haven't seen him, and you weren't expecting him! I know, it does sound crazy, but don't hang up. Yes, I was under the impression he was with you, but there isn't time just now to go into it. Maybe you can help. Wait, I've got someone else here to speak to you." She held out the receiver to George, her hand over the mouthpiece. "Nothing, of course! He isn't there. She knows nothing about him. But he *did* ring from a house, not from a box."

"From there, you may be sure." George took the line. "Mrs Mason? Superintendent Felse here. No, no cause for alarm, I merely called in here to talk to the boy again, in case he had anything to add to what he's already told us. Obviously you'll have gathered he's mislaid for the moment, but as he seems to have arranged French leave himself, I'd write it off as a rather inconsiderate prank on his part. But in the circumstances we'd naturally prefer to run him to earth as soon as possible. I believe your boy's a class-mate of his. Do you think I could have a word with Philip? He may just have overheard something at school that will give us a lead. I won't frighten him."

Philip came on the line sounding already considerably scared. Better make the questions such that he need only answer in monosyllables, the mother would undoubtedly be listening.

"Philip, you can help, if you will. All

280

I want to know is whether Bossie Jarvis telephoned home from your house this afternoon, an hour or two after school ended. He did? Yes, I know, he asked if he could, and you let him, that's all right, why shouldn't you? And your mother wasn't in, I guess? She'd gone to the library — yes, I see. Did you hear what Bossie had to say when he rang up? No, never mind, just tell me if I've got it right. He said he was staying overnight with you, to go to a party, so they wouldn't expect him home at all until tomorrow after school. Is that it? And he made you promise not to say a word — I know! All you need tell your mother is simply that you let him use the 'phone when he asked. But tell me this, did he tell you anything about what he was really going to do? All right, I believe you." It was what he would have expected. Bossie wouldn't confide his fell purposes to anyone unnecessarily. His own special bunch, accomplices at all times, were another matter. "Now you hand over to your mother again, and stop worrying. You've done all you can to help us now." And to the concerned and suspicious mother he said cheerfully: "Thank you, Mrs Mason, I'm sorry we had to bother you. Don't let Philip distress himself, he simply let his friend call home from your house when he asked. Quite natural, and not at all his fault if it was for a wrong purpose."

He might have some explaining to do, though, about why he hadn't mentioned doing Bossie that simple favour. That was his worry, however one might sympathise with him. George held on to the telephone after he had cut the call.

"Mind if I go ahead, Sam? Philip knows nothing beyond the fact that he span you a yarn to cover up something else he wanted to do. Hullo Jack? George Felse here. You know young Bossie's gang better than I do. Get up here and round up any of 'em you can get hold of. Wait, I'll get the list from Sam, I'm calling from his place. Sam, did he mention who was going with him on this abbey trip?"

Sam named them, the first faithful few Bossie had named. George relayed the information briskly. "I'll stay here on call until you find at least one of 'em.

The thing is, we've lost Bossie. He laid a smoke-screen — yes, quite definitely of intent — to cover a night's absence. No one knows where he is, not until you collar Ginger or one of the others. Get with it!"

"I'm gone," said Sergeant Moon, and hung up without a single question. George called the Mottisham Abbey number, which by this time at night would ring only in the caretaker's flat in the lodge. But there was no answer from John Stubbs.

"He probably makes a complete round at night," said Sam, straining to catch the distant, insistent ringing. "He may be the other side of the grounds. And we don't *know* that's where Bossie's likely to be."

"Yes," said Toby, "we do. The whole day has been his show. That parchment of his came from there, and he was the only one who knew it, and if that gang went there today, it was because he gave the orders."

Sam said ruefully: "He said they were planning a special project."

"You can say that again!" agreed Toby.

"But it was Bossie's project, and *very* special. Shouldn't we just go straight down there, Mr Felse?"

"Wait till we hear from Jack Moon first. But I'll get someone to go in from the station at Comerford."

And after that they waited, all of them, even Barbara and Willie the Twig too involved to break away, all waiting for Sergeant Moon to come up with one of Bossie's chorister-gangsters, and prise his general's secrets out of him. Jenny, white-faced but grimly composed, sat nursing the musical box that contained a tiny china shepherd, complete with ribboned crook and angelic lambs, and plays 'The Shepherd on the Rock', though she had quite forgotten that she was clutching it as if it had been a charm to retain hold of her own strayed lamb.

★ ★ ★

It was a quarter of an hour before Sergeant Moon called back, which seemed an age, though actually it was good going, in view of what he had to report.

"Believe it or not, yours isn't the

only missing lad tonight. It's infectious. Ginger Gibbs came late for his tea, moped around an hour or so, and has since disappeared. No panic there yet, he often goes off on his own ploys until getting on for ten, but his folks don't know where to look for him. Spuggy Price has also made off again, and being a couple of years younger he is expected to be in before now, and they're getting annoyed about it. Gwen the Shop says her Bill and those two, and maybe Jimmy Grocott, too, she thinks she heard his voice, had their heads together in her store-shed at the back, round about half past seven. Since then she hasn't seen any of them. But I've run one to earth for you finally — little Tom Rogers. He wasn't at the meeting in Gwen's shed, but he was with the gang this afternoon. Seems they all went round Mottisham Abbey together, and after they came out, Bossie said he was going to get in and have a hunt round during the night. He wouldn't let anybody else stay, but they saw him in through the fence up the back lane before they quit. Tom thinks they must have got more and more worried about it after they got home, and made up their minds they must go back, and either fetch him away or stand by him. That'll be Ginger, is my guess. Got the germ of a conscience. Anyhow, this lad's pretty sure that's where they'll all be. You don't want Tom, do you? I know everything he knows, now."

"No, send him home to bed. We've got enough of them on our hands. We're on our way down. If you get there before us, see if you can locate the warden for me, and hang on to him if you do find him. There's no getting in touch with him by 'phone so far. Nobody's answering."

"Stubbs?" Sergeant Moon took that up sharply. "That's interesting, because I got a flash from Brice in Birmingham, just before you called me out. He's been following up all the connections there, and came up with a nice little item on Stubbs. Before he came to this job at the abbey, and started frequenting the Rainbows, it seems he was courting steady in the city. Young woman in the antiques business. Dropped her after he got in with Rainbow on his home ground, and clapped eyes on Mrs Rainbow. You've got it! — before that he was mashing the Lavery girl!"

★ ★ ★

"Toby, come with me," said George. "You know the exact place Bossie'll be after. Sam, I know you'll want to be on hand, too."

"I'm coming," said Jenny firmly, and put down the musical box gently on the hall table, astonished to find her fingers stiff and bloodless when they released their hold.

"We'll be enough, Jenny. No panic now, we know where he is, we'll go and get him."

"We don't know it'll be that simple. We don't know what he's set in motion. You know him! I want to be there."

"You come on down after us with Barbara and Willie, then." He caught Barbara's eye, saw the glance she exchanged with Willie, and knew that he was understood. The Land-Rover would be driven down to Mottisham at an unwontedly sedate pace, and parked discreetly away from the main action, in the hope that by that time Bossie would have been hauled out of hiding safe and sound. Not that Jenny was a hysterical type, far from it; but once already her infant prodigy had almost got himself murdered, and parents are apt to over-react to that sort of thing.

"Come on, then!" said George, and led the way out to his own car at a run, with Toby and Sam on his heels. The greater their start, the better.

The night was dark, moonless and overcast. Traffic was always light up here at night, and the sense of the border hills closed in even on lighted roads, like the shadow of history, age-old and solitary and quite unmoved.

"Now suppose you tell me," suggested Sam, with arduous calm, "just what you know about all this business that we don't know." And Toby told him the reason for Bossie's misplaced loyalty. Apart from that they were all silent until they turned into the lane that led to the gates of the abbey, when Toby suddenly said aloud: "I wish now I'd never touched the bloody thing!"

"Oh, come off it!" said Sam comfortingly.

"I wish I had a quid for every time I've said something like that. What makes you think you should be any different? "

★ ★ ★

There was one police car waiting for them, as well as Sergeant Moon's ancient Ford. The portion of the drive between the old entrance gates and the ticket-kiosk was still shrouded in its overgrown trees and shrubs, and hid unusual activities very efficiently. Jack Moon came out of the darkness to meet them as they climbed out of the car.

"I sent a couple of the lads round to look for the place where the kid got in. We've got it pinned and covered now, if he slips out that way. We've made no other move yet."

"And Stubbs still isn't around?" The resident warden was no scholar himself, his orders as regards the work in hand came from Charles Goddard, but his responsibility for the site, like his authority within it, was absolute, and he should have been there. "What are his free nights, do we know?"

"We do," said Moon flatly. "On Wednesday, Thursday and Friday he can be away the entire day if he likes, but he's responsible for security from six o'clock on. Saturday and Sunday evenings he has a relief to make the evening rounds, so he's free from closing time. The rest of the week he's in sole charge, apart from the help he gets during the day, which is voluntary but usually plentiful. This is Tuesday, and he should be here. He may be, but if he is, he's taking a hell of a time over making the round of the property. It's big, but not that big."

"With or without him," said George, "we're going in."

"That's what I thought, so I fetched Grainger along with me." Grainger was the best man in the Midshire force on locks, and happened to live in Moon's territory. "The telephone switchboard is in the ticket-office, we're going to need that, and of course the office is locked. Even if Stubbs is off with the keys to everything in his pocket, there should be a second set in there somewhere. Has he got your authority to break in?"

"As fast as possible," said George

without hesitation, and led the way. Authorisation could be legalised afterwards.

"History repeats itself," murmured Toby, following, and shook his shoulders to dislodge a foreboding that was not so easy to jettison. "Well, *I* got out again all right!"

9

BOSSIE was relieved but vaguely disquieted when he tried the door at the corner of the northern walk, to find that, like the gate, it was still unlocked. But after all, there was nothing here to steal, nothing profitable even from the point of view of an antique dealer, except the tiles in the flooring, and it was doubtful if they carried a great commercial value. Dispersed from their proper site, they were just moderately-priced antiquarian junk. *In situ* they were treasure. And nobody was going to bring a fleet of pantechnicons and remove the stable block en masse.

Once inside, he eased the latch softly back into its cradle, and stood for a moment in the vast darkness, sensible of the shape it took, feeling his hair erected by the soaring of the timbered roof, and his vision channelled into the form of its noble length, closed in on either side, on his left by the eighteenth-century brickwork with its high, small windows that hardly showed at all for relief against the dark, on his right by the huge, decrepit stone wall that had survived at least six hundred years. Under that wall his membrane had been found, lying among the growth of grass and weeds nurtured on years of rubble, dust and moisture. And he was sure now that it had been one among many, very many, and could not by any accident have been winnowed far enough away from its fellows to be discovered in absolute solitude. And nobody else had even made similar finds here, or they would have been written up for everybody to read, and photographed and made much of. No, the secret was here, somewhere, however obscurely hidden. He was certain.

When he had stood still long enough to have his breathing under control, and to be sure he was really alone, he switched on his torch. The long vista of the north walk opened before him, the ancient vaulting gone, the complex timbering of the later roof making a shadowy pattern overhead. The stones of the north wall showed wonderfully jagged and crude in the cross-light, and at their foot the earth flooring, swept bare and trodden hard, looked the least likely hiding-place for secrets that he could imagine. He walked its length, searching the angle of floor with wall, and could see no possible place where anything could have been hidden from those who had done this thorough job of cleaning the ground.

Bossie drew back and viewed the whole. There was a quantity of stuff, old wood, fragments of carved, weathered stone retrieved from various places about the site, rope and twine, all piled in the far corner, together with a handcart and some brushes and brooms. Nothing there to conceal treasure, though they might, if necessary, conceal somebody who wanted to be invisible here. Then there was the area of relaid paving tiles, inside the ropes, and a heap of excavated tiles, some whole, some broken, waiting to be assembled into the pattern, after due repairs.

And outside everything, wherever he turned the tiny beam of his torch, the huge, impersonal darkness, distorted by enormous shadows that dwarfed the little light, and a smell of disturbed earth, like a cemetery. It was getting distinctly chilly, too, he felt himself shivering.

Well, if there had been anything concealed in the upper layers here, in the centre, where they were working on the tiling, they would certainly have found it. No need to disturb anything there. All that remained was the wall itself, and the flooring under it, which was certainly where Toby had found his leaf, even if it didn't look very promising now.

He was working his way methodically along the rim of the roped-off area, where the earth flooring was excavated to a depth of about three inches, and the raw edges at least offered a possibility that a corner of parchment might show among the soil and gravel, when a sudden small sound caused the hair to rise on the nape of his neck, and sent him diving into the corner behind the hand-cart, his torch hastily extinguished. The grate of a key in the lock might have alerted him more rapidly, but the door was not locked, and what he heard was the neat click of the latch yielding, and without even a full second in between, the door swung silently open. It was new, light and noiseless; it ought to have been heavy, creaky and slow, to give him time to make the best of his inadequate cover. But if this was simply a routine round, there would be the merest flick of a torch round the interior, and then the warden would move on, satisfied.

Bossie had miscalculated, owing to inadequate data. The careful restorers of the paving, salvaging broken tiles from under layers of soil, matching and repairing and patiently assembling the fours into their patterns of coiled leaves and tendrils, had sometimes worked both early and late, and fitted up for their needs a highly efficient temporary lighting system, which was not used during show hours. Of all the things to which Bossie was blind, the marvels of technical efficiency came at the head of the list. Probably Ginger could have told him the place was wired for a perfect blaze of light, but Bossie had noticed nothing, neither the switch by the door nor the dangling bulbs all along the north walk. And the flood of light that suddenly sprang up overhead almost flattened him into the floor with its unexpected force. Crude white light that threaded through the wheels of the handcart, probed behind the stacked wood, and reduced the derelict stones to unhelpful pebbles. Light crashed down on his head and pressed him to his knees, but he knew at once that if this person in the doorway came on into the room, he could not possibly avoid being seen. His heart stopped for one frightful instant, and then sturdily picked up its beat. Being scared was no protection whatever, he might as well go on breathing, after all. There could be credible, if not respectable, reasons for being here at this hour.

"Well, well!" said a familiar voice, mild, amused, even teasing. "This is really excess of enthusiasm. I gathered you were a devotee, but don't you think this is carrying it to absurd lengths? Oh, do come on out of there! You might as well, I can see you perfectly, and I don't get one like you every trip. I've recognised you already, and you don't look at all comfortable."

Bossie wasn't comfortable, and besides, he had recognised the intruding voice as quickly as its possessor had recognised him, and the relief was enormous. Not the warden, after all, but the nice guide who had been so patient and accommodating in showing them round in the afternoon. In any case, Bossie's dignity was affronted at crouching behind a hand-cart in full view of an eye-witness. He rose to his full unimpressive height, and came out from behind his barricade. The big, fair-haired, amiable young man grinned at him from just within the doorway, and made no intimidating move to approach nearer.

"Well, now I've seen everything! I've known kids driven in here in a state of mutiny, but I've never before known one come back for more out of hours. You've made my day. But I shudder to think what you're laying up for yourself. Do you realise it's getting on for ten? Your parents must be worried sick about you. Whatever possessed you to hide away in here like this?"

He sounded just as he had sounded in the afternoon, patient, tolerant and amused, and that gave him every right to take the mickey, in his airy way. Bossie drew a little nearer, cautiously but placatingly.

"I wasn't going to steal anything, or do any damage. But did you know there are stories that the last prior buried the church plate and treasures somewhere here? I wanted to try and find them, make some fabulous discovery and get to be famous. But if I'd found anything, I should have told!"

"I'm sure you would," agreed the guide with amusement, and studying him very attentively. "Well, that's all very nice, I dare say, and no doubt places like this ought to be bulging with buried treasure all over the shop. But we've exhausted the possibilities in this part, you know, and you are rather wasting your time. As well as frightening your folks half to death, I could think. And just as well for you it happens to be me making the rounds tonight, and not the warden, he'd have you frog-marched up to the police station in no time flat. You be thankful he wanted to go out tonight, and I volunteered to do the locking up for him."

"Oh, I am!" agreed Bossie fervently. "But I didn't mean to do anything wrong, really, and I didn't realise it was as late as all that."

"I should think not! Do you realise you could have got yourself locked in here overnight? That would have scared them even worse, and I don't suppose you'd have been feeling quite so cocky yourself when it got really cold. So now hadn't you better tell me where you live, and let me drive you safely home? And don't blame me if you get your behind tanned when you get there!"

That was when Bossie made his great mistake, and after that there was no salvaging it. Obviously he couldn't let himself be driven home, having accounted for a night's absence, or in the stress of the moment he had no time to realise that that would now have been his safest and sanest course, however many awkward explanations it might involve. He never gave up his enterprises easily; and before he had time to think he heard himself politely declining this fair offer.

"That's awfully kind of you, really, but you see I'm staying with some friends for tonight, here in Mottisham. So my people won't be worrying about me. But thank you, all the same. It's only five minutes' walk."

There was a brief and deep silence. The guide did not move from his position with his back against the door, and his eyes narrowed thoughtfully upon the small, stolid figure before him, though he continued to smile and speak with amused resignation.

"It is, is it? And home, I suppose, is somewhere a good deal further away. But surely *somebody* must be wanting to know where you're prowling at ten o'clock at night? What sort of friends do your parents have, if they let you run wild to this hour?"

Bossie floundered in deeper in his haste, and felt the morass of all too detectable fibs tugging at his feet, but it was too late to draw back. "Oh, they weren't expecting me very early, because I told them I should be coming late from my music lesson."

"About three hours late, I imagine," said the young man drily.

He ought to have known. He could see

all the flaws himself. A twelve-year-old's music lesson would be arranged for a civilised hour like half past six or seven. He'd given himself away completely. It wouldn't take a genius to conclude that he was lying about his night's lodging, and it wasn't a long step from that to concluding positively that he had so played off the two ends against each other as to leave his parents convinced he was safe with a known host in Mottisham, while the supposed host had no notion whatever that he was anywhere but in his own bed at home. In short, nobody knew where he was, or what he was doing . . .

The fair young man heaved a philosophical sigh, smiled at him even more benevolently, and reaching a hand into his pocket, drew out a bunch of keys, and selected the right one with a flick of long fingers. Silently he closed the door, and moving aside for the first time, turned the key, and locked them in together.

Perhaps the act in itself would have been enough, but it was what the act revealed that hit Bossie like a lightning-stroke. For a moment he stopped breathing, frozen with shock. The flooding light that had blazed down on them all this while now fell for the first time directly on the right hand that was so deliberately turning the key, and on the third finger of that hand was a large, flattish seal-ring made from a black stone like an onyx or a very dark moss agate. He had seen just that motion and just that flat flash from the polished blackness once before, and had failed to remember and identify it. Among the tangle of tombs under the church tower that same hand, wearing the same ring, had turned up Rainbow's limp head to the light of a torch. No other part of the nocturnal marauder had been lit like that. Now the turn of the long muscular hand echoed the same gesture, and memory recovered from the paralysis of shock. He didn't know who this man was, but he knew all too well *what* he was. He was Rainbow's murderer.

And he, Bossie, was locked in with him, and like a fool he had brought it on himself. If only he'd jumped at the offer to drive him home, maybe snivelled a little and repented of his adventure, this man might have been reassured that he knew nothing, had nothing to tell, could never identify him; and he might have done just what he had offered, driven him home and stopped worrying about him. Which would have been his mistake. But now Bossie was the one who'd made the mistake. There was only one thing he hadn't betrayed, and that was that all five of his companions of the afternoon knew very well where he was, and could tell the police as soon as it dawned on somebody that something was wrong. If he dropped that out now, casually, or deliberately and with obvious intent, would he be believed? And would it make any difference now? No, it was too late. If he'd blabbed all that like a scared kid right at the beginning, it might have worked, his captor might have decided it was too dangerous to make away with him, and returned to his role of tolerant Dutch-uncle. Not now! He'd watched the door being closed, and the murderer had watched his face as he took in the significance of the act. It would take more than a sudden story of five potential witnesses to undo that. Even if he was believed, it would only hasten whatever was going to happen, to get him out of the way at once, and Bossie was pretty sure he was in no hurry to get on with it.

Which left only the delaying tactics of gormless, childish stupidity, innocence almost incredible. Notice nothing, admit nothing, remain trustingly ingenuous, not to say imbecile.

He shuffled his feet uneasily, and crossed his eyes, as he could do at will, though he never knew when he did it involuntarily. "I'm sorry, it wasn't really true, that stuff I told you. I shouldn't have tried to fool my parents like that. Maybe I ought to go home, after all. I only wanted to explore . . . I did tell them I was going to stay with Philip Mason, I've often done it before, so they won't be anxious. But it wasn't right, was it? You know, I'm ever so glad you came. I don't really like this place, after all, not now it's dark . . . " Bossie could raise a tear just as nimbly as he could raise a fist, and produced a heart-rending contortion of a face never notable for beauty, as well as a genuine

305

trickle down his cheek. And all the while he knew it wasn't any good. His brains did show so plainly!

They were working frantically now. He was sure this man knew the name James Jarvis, and his address, from the Locke anthem he had lost in the churchyard, but did he know what James Jarvis looked like? At least he'd gone to the trouble to find out Bossie's routine, enough to hunt him down on his way home from the music lesson. But there might still be room for confusion. To some people all kids of about the same age looked alike. Who else of comparable age lived up that same road?

"Would you really take me home?" he bleated hopefully. "I'm Adrian Bowen, my dad lives at the Moor Farm in Abbot's Bale. I don't care if I do get into trouble, I want to go home!" If a miracle happened, and he was believed and duly delivered there, the Bowens would at any rate haul him into the house, if only to demand explanations, and it would be too late then to drag him out again by force. But he didn't believe in it! He worked at it, but he knew he was up against a stone wall. Solider than the one now flanking them!

The man leaning back against the door never moved, never took his eyes from Bossie, and as yet said no word. His smile had vanished, he peered from beneath brows drawn and morose, almost irritable, and jutted a thoughtful lower lip as he wrestled with this problem. But the false name did not make the slightest impression on his fierce concentration.

"And for a while there you almost had me fooled," he mused at last, as much to himself as to Bossie. "Why the hell did you have to go and get mixed up in this business? Why did you meddle? You're the one who's made this necessary, you know that?" Downright accusingly, as if Bossie owed him an abject apology for forcing his hand like this to a repugnant act. What am I going to do with you now?" he demanded, in tones decidedly aggrieved.

"You could drive me home, like you offered," sniffed Bossie, determinedly obtuse. But the disguise was thinning; what was the use of it, if it was ineffective?

"Knowing as much as you know, James Boswell Jarvis?" said his enemy, and heaved his broad shoulders with an effort away from the door, and took a long stride forward into the north walk. "Not bloody likely!"

★ ★ ★

"Your show, Toby," said George, marshalling his handful of men within the barrier, and casting a glance aside at the ticket-office, where a uniformed constable had taken over the switchboard and re-established contact with the system, and was at this moment engaged in the first of a series of calls designed to run to earth the truant warden of Mottisham Abbey, who apparently had all available keys with him, since they had found none in the office. "Lead on, you know where Bossie's liable to have holed up."

In the complex of buildings, gardens, excavations and reserves of plant and scaffolding, Toby moved with cautious speed. Things had changed since last he gate-crashed this enclosure.

"The stable-block's this way." He went

ahead steadily, and brought them face to face with the long line of the eighteenth-century wall. The night remained dark, and George had thought it best to work as far as possible without lights, using torches only fleetingly where necessary. He had given no voice to his misgivings, but Toby had grasped that the absence of John Stubbs was a matter for anxiety. He was one of the names against which a question-mark reared, he was here conveniently installed on the spot, and he was not where, by the terms of his appointment, he should have been. Moreover, he had been absent now for a length of time which should have allowed him to make the round of his charge, and be back at his post, but there was still no sign of him.

The gate that guarded the archway was closed, but yielded to a touch. The key was not in the lock. Toby pushed the gate open and slid through, with George and Sergeant Moon at his heels, and turned right, to make for the door in the north-east corner of the yard. And there he halted at the first step. The range of small, high windows in the inner wall of the north range glowed hollowly with a steady but muted light, reflected from below and patterned with shadows from the network of roof rafters.

"There's somebody — " began Toby, low-voiced, and bit off the rest as George laid a warning hand on his arm. For there was indeed somebody within there, and though it might be Bossie, was it likely that a boy playing the secret investigator by night would run the risk of betraying his presence by switching on a whole array of lights, in a place where he had no right to be? Not a boy as bright as Bossie!

George went forward alone, moving silently along the wall to the door, beneath which a very thin line of light showed. He grasped the handle, and very gingerly turned it, but it did not yield to pressure. Locked! And locked with someone inside, and the lights on.

Correction, with two people inside. For hollowly from within he heard voices.

"What the hell can you expect, now you've put me in this position?" The once-amiable and encouraging guide looked a very different person now,

310

coming forward slow step by step, glaring annoyance and genuine resentment from under brows tight and creased as though in pain. "It's your own damned silly fault, you should have let well alone. You don't think I *like* having to do this, do you?"

"You don't have to." Bossie was backing cautiously away along the rope, feeling his way. Not that it was going to do him much good even if he could dodge round to the other side and make a dash for the door, because he had watched his enemy withdraw and pocket the keys. "Nobody's making you do anything. And if you know what's good for you you won't try, because my friends who were here with me this afternoon are coming back for me. They'll be here any minute, you won't have time to get away."

"What a hope!" said his enemy with a tired and petulant smile. "You've made it clear enough that nobody knows where you are, and nobody's going to know where you disappear from. I've got plenty of time."

"That's where you're wrong. There are five of them who know exactly where I am, and if I don't show up again they're going to tell . . . "

He wasn't believed, of course. There was no way of making that story convincing now. And he had reached the place where the piled junk and the hand-cart narrowed the way, and was feeling his way blindly past the obstructions when his foot slipped over the edge of the excavated section, and slight though the drop was, it threw him off balance. He fell against the rope, and rolled under it, and then a large hand had him by the back of his blazer, hauled him upright, and slammed him against the stone wall, and its fellow was clamped over his mouth just too late to suppress a single yell of indignation, rage and terror.

As if that one shout had set off a chain reaction of unnerving assaults upon the silence of the night, there was a sudden thunderous salvo of knocks on the locked door, a violent rattling of the handle, and a peremptory voice ordering: "Open up in there! This is the police! We're here in force, you can't get away. Unlock this door!"

* * *

Silence again, absolute silence. No querulous baritone and no reedy, wavering treble to be heard now inside the long room, not the least sound of movement or even breathing. Outside the door George leaned with an ear against the wood, straining to hear if any indication of struggle or distress stirred within, but there was nothing. Behind him Sam and Toby stood painfully still.

Presently George began to talk, clearly, reasonably, deliberately, without haste.

"We know you're in there now. We know the boy is with you. We know there's no one else in there. Whatever happens to him will be your doing, no one else's. Your responsibility. Think about it! What a fool you'd be to harm him now! You can't get away. Touch him, and you destroy yourself. Only the desperate do that, and why should your case be desperate? You're a reasoning man, you can see what's in your own best interests. It's only a matter of time, why prolong it? You may as well open the door now, it will make no difference

313

in the end, and spare you and us a great deal of trouble. Mitigating circumstances always count."

Between sentences he waited, but still silence, never a word in reply. A slightly less intense silence and stillness in there, perhaps, the faint suggestion of slight movements, of people breathing, even the stealthy suggestion of furious thought. But no words.

"If you harm that boy, you're done for, you understand that, don't you? Up to now you're not in any desperate case, are you? But there'd be no shadow of doubt about that, and you'd pay for it to the limit. Why not see reason? To start with, prove you haven't harmed him already. That will be something in your favour. Let him speak! Just enough to say: Yes, I'm here, yes, I'm all right. Bossie, are you listening?"

If there was the kind of response a gagged mouth can make, it was barely loud enough to reach the listeners straining their ears outside the door, but there was something else, a sudden sharp crack, as though a foot had back-heeled stone, and then a suppressed gasp and the brief flutter of a very unequal struggle, instantly suppressed. Then silence again.

"Get Grainger." said George in a whisper, and one of the constables slipped away. "Jack, take a look at those windows — though I think they're too high and too small to be any use. And, Sam, could you bear to go back to Jenny, and try to keep her there, out of this? Leave us to do what can be done, you know we'll stick at nothing to get him out. You look after Jenny."

"Yes, I'll go." There was nothing Sam had been able to do so far but stand and listen and suffer. And if nobody told Jenny anything pretty soon, she'd be coming to find out. He felt his way quietly along the wall to the archway, and departed.

"He *is* there," Toby whispered. "I think he's still OK. He couldn't use his tongue, but he used his feet. That's Bossie! He won't hurt him now, surely! What good would it do him?"

None, true enough. But these cases who get themselves into a state of siege, with hostages, sometimes take their revenge on the world that way. It made no sense, no. Bossie might be more than half the case against Rainbow's murderer, if it came to a charge, but where that left the killer at least a chance of acquittal and freedom after trial, killing Bossie now would leave him no chance at all. But that was an argument of reason, not of spite, and spite can argue, too. All they could do was go on talking to him in reasonable terms, urging his best interests on him, talking him into exhaustion, if need be, but never into frenzy.

"All right, we can afford to wait. You can't get away. But what are you gaining? You may as well come out now, and spare yourself some uncomfortable hours. We're patient people, we shan't tire and go away."

Sergeant Grainger came, placidly muting his skeleton keys, a big man stepping as lightly as a cat. And hard on his heels came Barbara and Willie the Twig, asking no questions, already apprised of what was happening. That was an idea! Perhaps Barbara's voice, coming unexpectedly, might jolt the young man within out of another fragment of confidence and resolution, make him

316

more amenable to reason, if not to resignation. George drew her aside to let Grainger come to the lock.

"Barbara, we're going in, and I want to keep the operation covered and his attention distracted while we deal with the lock. You try talking to him, he's not expecting you," Getting in might be a ticklish moment, but they would have to play it as cautiously as possible, no rushing their quarry into panic.

She asked in a whisper: "Is it John Stubbs?"

"Seems so. He's nowhere else to be found. Try it! Keep talking gently till we get through."

Her voice was one of her particular beauties, deep, clear, slightly husky, an admirer could never mistake it for any other. She stood pressed against the hinged side of the door while Grainger worked, handling his tools gently, without a sound, until metal edged metal inside the lock.

"John, is that really you in there? This is Barbara. John, that's a friend of mine you've got in there with you, and I want him safe, you wouldn't do anything to

317

hurt him, would you? I've got a present for him that he hasn't even seen yet. I don't know how you got into this mess, John, I thought I knew you, at least a little. I still think so, and this isn't your style at all." She would have liked to pause and listen to the quality of the continued but subtle silence within, for it seemed to be passing through as many changes as the inflections of speech, but she could not break the thread, because of the tiny sounds of metal on metal, engaging and slipping, and gripping again. "Don't go on with this, what's the point of hurting people more? What good can that do you or anyone? Open the door and come out to us now. Send Bossie out to me. And then you come. I'll be here waiting for you, I promise."

The sergeant made a fine, satisfied sound, and she heard the lock surrender and the handle turn, easing wood softly a fraction of an inch from wood. A hair-fine line of light showed. George put her gently aside, and thrust the door wide open.

At the far end of the long room, just

short of the corner where the hand-cart and its attendant fragments lay, two figures clamped tightly together stood backed against the stone wall. In front Bossie, with his own handkerchief thrust between his teeth and knotted tightly behind his head, his glasses askew, and a coil of rough baling twine spiralling tightly from his waist to his shoulders, pinioning his arms. The last length of the cord was looped round his neck, tightly enough to score the skin, and behind him, gripping the end of the loop and glaring fury and desperation, stood, not John Stubbs but Colin Barron.

10

THE voice that came jerking out of him, after so long of obstinate silence, was loud, harsh and too high-pitched. "Take one step in here and I kill him! One step, that's enough!"

Nobody moved. Frozen in the doorway, they measured the odds, and found them impossible. The room was long. By the time even the fleetest of them reached him, he could kill, and by the look of his face, that sharp, easy, knowing, business face hardly recognisable now in its pale ferocity, he would kill. Even the convulsive tension of his fingers was tightening the cord as they watched. One false move, and it would be over. The sweat running on his forehead was clearly visible in the flooding light.

"Don't touch that light switch! Don't put a hand near it! If you do, he's dead for a start. I shan't need light to finish him off."

Carefully unmoving, George said in a

flat, neutral voice: "Why go on? Turn him loose and come with us, you'll be sparing yourself worse things. At least talk. And listen."

"I'll talk to you through the door, if I talk at all. Get back out of here, leave the light, and close the door. Or I'll kill him, If you try anything, I'll make sure he goes first."

With aching care, inch by inch, hands in full view to show nothing was contemplated against him, they withdrew. They left the light on, they closed the door.

Back to square one! Not John Stubbs, but Colin Barron, the smart young dealer who thought it well worth while poking his nose in wherever Rainbow turned his attention, the one who had followed him up into Middlehope, found some profitable business with the sale of the Macsen-Martel effects, but never quite discovered Rainbow's real incentive, and was constantly, inquisitively on the prowl after it. And had he ever really coveted Barbara, or merely made use of her, or tried to, as she had been employed to make use of him and his kind? Not a pleasant world! No wonder she had recoiled from it to the remotest extremes of Middlehope Forest.

Barbara stood in monumental, frowning calm, fronting the closed door. Possibly the same thoughts were in her mind. She raised her voice to carry clearly within.

"Colin? Are you listening? I'm sorry I called you John. You dropped him in the muck, you see, hauling off like this. I don't say I was ever sure about you, Colin, but I may have thought you all sorts of things, but never a coward. Men don't fight behind children, Colin. Only apologies for men. Now prove which you are. Give us Bossie, and I'll get back my respect for you. What are you gaining by threatening him, anyhow? If we can't get in, you can't get out. Never, not on your terms. You'd better start considering ours. Just tell me, as a matter of academic interest, did you ever really think anything of me? It would be interesting to know."

She was never going to know, of course, because what could she or anyone make of that sudden, strangling, sobbing outburst of sexual profanity that bubbled behind the door. One might gather that she was a married whore, and he a winnowing wind blowing both her and her proprietor-husband where he listed, but the mixture of abuse and longing no one was ever going to disentangle. Happily only she, rather than Bossie, seemed to be threatened by this storm. Barbara was drawing some very dangerous fire. The vibrations from within sounded enfeebled rather than intensified.

"I tell you what," called Barbara, irrepressible in inspiration, "sell us Bossie for me! You do realise you can trade him, don't you? If you feel that way about me, here I am, put your contemptible noose about my neck instead. I shall be a volunteer, and I'm over twenty-one, Colin. Think how much better that will make you feel!"

It was more than enough. Willie the Twig took her by the arm and drew her away into the open, chilly, clean centre of the courtyard, and she understood and accepted his suggestion that she had pushed things to the safe limit, and made her point that Bossie, alive, was a valuable bargaining counter. She went where Willie led her, quivering. She wound her arms about his neck and pressed her lips into his throat, and it was a motion of exultation rather than a gesture of heed or appeal.

"It's all right," said Willie into her ear, "it's all right! He isn't crazy, his mind's working, you got to him, all right."

All the same, it was back to stalemate. Back to: "We're still here, Barron. We shan't go away, you know that. And you can't, not without us. There's no way on this earth you can get out of there except in our arms. So why prolong it? Mrs Rainbow is right. The boy is quite irrelevant. We can't get in, but you can't get out. And we, in the long run, don't have to get in, but you, in the end, do have to get out. Walking or carried, alive or dead, there's only this one way out for you, and we're not quitting. Think it over, Barron! Make it as easy on yourself as possible. Come out now!"

It went on and on, monotonously. Moon taking a turn, George returning to the attack, a barrage of voice's kept up relentlessly to leave him no time to relax, no time to think or despair, in case despair should take it's worst course. But somehow he had made time to think, all the same. Now that he'd begun to talk, and knew his identity was known, he used his voice with increasing aggression. Not confidence, perhaps, a kind of last-ditch bravado.

"You want this kid, Felse? Intact? I've got the goods. I put the price on them, understand?" Barbara had reached him, sure enough.

"No harm in naming your price," agreed George. "The customer doesn't have to buy. Not when he has a foreclosure on you in the end, in any case. But go on talking, we're listening."

"Don't forget the seller can chuck the goods in the dustbin if he doesn't get his price. You'd better listen. If I don't get the return I want, I can still wipe him out."

"That would settle your own hash, and you know it. I don't think you're crazy enough to want that."

"I might be, Felse, I might be, if there's nothing else left. There's no hanging now.

And there's a lot better remission than you lot like, and even parole — What should I be, by comparison with some of the real killers? Just one kid, and almost cleanly!"

It was curious that the more ghastly his arguments became, the more secure seemed Bossie's future. He was very seriously beginning to consider his captive as a barterable commodity, not to be squandered. George had visions of having to rouse the Chief Constable in the middle of the night.

"Go on, I'm interested. What do you want, a jet plane to fly you to Libya?"

"I'll get myself out of the country, there are ways. Nothing as ambitious as that. I want all your men called off for twelve hours, and a car brought here for me — and my little nephew, of course!"

"A dark green SAAB?" asked George. "The one you used to try and run him down? You'll have to prove he's still as good as new, first, you realise that? Nobody buys a pig in a poke."

"A nice, well-maintained police car, with everything legitimate, and twelve hours' guarantee of a clean bill, in case of any hitch. And he's OK as of now, and I'll prove it if I have to, but he won't be, if you bitch me up short of noon tomorrow."

"On the other hand," pointed out George, tirelessly mild, "you are still stuck in there, the one who needs clemency. Unless you convince us we have to, we are not disposed to let you out, except into our custody. You'd better be a lot more convincing."

A sudden, prolonged, tired but vicious outburst of profanity. No detectable movement, no struggle at all, things getting bedded down into a status quo. No, he wouldn't slaughter his bargaining counter. Given time, he might even fall asleep from exhaustion. But he was a tough proposition, far tougher than John Stubbs, with any amount of stamina.

It was no comfort at all when the constable from the switchboard made his way in just after eleven, to announce in a triumphant whisper: "We've found him! Stubbs! He's in Birmingham, at this Lavery woman's flat, seems they had a dinner date on the town, and he jumped at it when this chap Barron offered to do his evening rounds for him. Some of the students wanted to stay on late and finish charting the bit of infirmary they were working on, and Barron said he'd see them off the premises and lock up. We called the flat several times before, but they were still out. They're only just back. He's on his way back here now."

Poor harmless, glum, undecided John Stubbs, good enough to run a job like this caretaking one at Mottisham, but not good enough to get much higher on his own achievements, jealous and resentful of smarter acquaintances such as Colin Barron, but willing to lean on them, too. And torn between two grotesquely different women, and the mixed fortunes they offered, salvation to the undistinguished. So all the time he was taking the more profitable legatee out to dinner! In crass innocence!

"You still there, Felse?" demanded the hoarse, vindictive voice from within.

"I'm still here. I'm listening."

"Better make up your mind quickly, if you want this kid, I'm getting tired of waiting. Give me the break I want, and he's yours."

"If you turn him loose to us here on the spot, that might be worth considering. But it doesn't rest with me, and there are no short cuts to an answer."

"Not a chance! I don't take my halter off him until I'm clear. Then I'll dump him safely, somewhere he can look after himself."

"And we should trust you? But you'd never make it, you know, I guarantee that. You'd much better come out, and get it over."

"If I don't make it, he doesn't make it, either. I'll see to that! So get to your damned Chief Constable, and get things moving. And I want more time, since you're wasting so much. I want a full day!"

If he was tiring, it didn't show in his voice. All those listening tried to find some sign of weakening, of wandering resolution, and couldn't. And nothing had changed; there was just this one way out and in, and parley with him was in fact only an exercise in wearing him down, and none too effective so far.

It was going to be a long night.

Toby couldn't stand still and listen to it any longer. He turned his back and groped away along the wall, out of the stable-yard, and round to the left, to circle the whole block and look once more for some other means of approach, anything that would turn the scale. Though he knew that Moon and the constables had already done the same thing, and found nothing of any use. It was better than standing outside the door thinking helplessly of Bossie inside there, roped into helplessness and with a noose round his neck, and of Jenny, with superhuman forbearance, keeping her distance as requested, and dying every minute.

A few broken, embedded stones of a wall jutted for some yards from the corner of the stable-block. He stumbled over them, and came round to the rear of the north walk of the old cloister, into the nave of the church. All along there on his left ran the thick, decrepit stone wall that once had severed the church from the cloister. And to his right the gardens fell away, and gave place to a large, cleared space, receding into darkness between distant walls, where some trick of latent and reflected light, owing to its white encrustations, showed him dimly the shape of a concrete mixer. The sky was a little paler than it had been, against it he could see the tracery of scaffolding encasing one wall, though it vanished again into a single darkness below the skyline. The workmen had much of their plant and stores here, it seemed.

Toby moved along the wall, his left hand extended to touch the rough and crumbling surface, and groped his way round a short, buttress-like projection, surely added long after the church itself was gone and the cloister had become stables. Sign enough that this wall, though immense, had been showing traces of disintegration even in the eighteenth century, and needed propping at this point. As he rounded it and felt for the wall again, a small figure erupted under his feet with a muted squeak of alarm, and instantly shushed imperiously at him, as if he had been the offender. Startled, Toby looked down into a round face just visible as a pallor in the night, and clutched at a coat-collar, and was himself as promptly and eagerly clutched by the arm, and towed away into the scaffolded and plant-stacked shelter of the distant buildings, away from the critical zone.

He went willingly, as soon as he had divined the reason; and the moment they were well away from the wall an intent voice round the region of his upper arm hissed at him: "Mister, I couldn't talk there, you can hear right through. That's Bossie he's got in there! We've got to get him out!"

"I know!" agreed Toby in the same urgent undertone. "We're trying to. It's full of police round there, but we can't get in. He's threatening to hurt Bossie if we do. Hey, you're Bossie's stand-in, aren't you? Spuggy?"

"Yes, we're all here, four of us. We had to come back. He told us not to, but we had to, we couldn't leave him on his own."

"Took long enough, didn't you?" complained Toby ungratefully, going blindly where he was urged, by a guide so close to the ground that he trod it as knowingly as a mouse.

"I know, we waited outside for a bit, and then we had to get into cover because the coppers came round there. They're watching the place now, they'd never have let us come in. We had to go a long way round, and we got a bit lost in the dark. But we've been here ages now, only we didn't know then what to do."

But now they did know? Marvellously, the small, fierce voice sounded sure of itself. Somebody had thought of something that could be done, and this mite was both spy to report the latest state of battle inside the north walk, and now recruiting sergeant for the cause. If a police constable had wandered round the corner he might have hesitated; any civilian was as good as in uniform. He hauled his prize in among the stacked timbers and scaffolding poles under the wing of the house, and three more shadows popped up to receive them. The tallest stood slightly higher than Toby's shoulder.

"There's a bloke here got a bit more weight," announced Spuggy tersely. "I think he's game."

The tallest of the nocturnal waifs eyed the larger shape dimly outlined, and said at once: "Eh, you're the chap who visits at Bossie's place, aren't you? Look, we've got to have some help. Where do we need the top-weight on this thing, fore or aft? For a ram?"

Toby peered at the ground, dropping to his knees to be sure of what was being offered him. A large, folding ladder, three-fold, and long at that, left here among the plant. Surely more than aluminium by its weight, some sort of stout alloy. By the size of it, it was meant to be strong, and its ends jutted formidably.

"For God's sake!" said Toby, awed. "That wall's heaven knows how thick."

"I know, but part of it's rotten as rubble," said Ginger, whose father had taught him about building. "We saw it inside, this afternoon, you could see daylight through. Look, you can see light through it now."

It was true. From this modest distance, and square to the affected area, Colin Barron's protective light shone through very clearly in several starry points, the weak joint in his armour.

"We were inside this afternoon. That part, it's just left of where they're standing. The wall bulges. I reckon it's ready to go if we hit it right."

"We might kill them," doubted Toby fearfully.

"There isn't any other way. We've got to try."

From the darkness under the house wall a hearty whisper blew into their colloquy like a gale-force wind. "You have positively got something there," owned Willie the Twig, coming round the concrete-mixer, "that I wish I'd thought of."

They knew him, and were not disconcerted; everybody knew Will Swayne could move among the wild things in the forest and never be detected unless he wished. And he was an ally after their own hearts. Where Willie was, Barbara would not be far away. Her scent was on the air, shadowy there at Willie's shoulder.

"Weight forward of amidships, I'd say, either side now we're two matched. You lot will have to gallop. And Barbie, make yourself useful, go back and tip off the police, they'll have to rush him the instant they hear us hit. In case!"

Barbara, glittering, whispered: "Yes!" as roused and resolute as the children, and turned and whisked away into the dark. "Give her two minutes," said Willie, "enough to pass the word, not enough for them to interfere." He lifted his side of the ladder, shifting back far enough to give it a prow calculated to do maximum damage before its crew reached the point of risk. Six of them now to man it, and the forward two could hoist most of its weight and balance it, while the lightest weights, Spuggy Price and Jimmy Grocott, manfully matched their small persons but immense pugnacity next in the line, and Toffee Bill and Ginger, the architect of the whole enterprise, brought up the rear with no spare length going to waste, and all their force behind the ram. It was all crazy and improvised and amateur, but at least it was action and thought, the sort of desperate sortie men might have mounted in the centuries when this place was first built.

The steady pattern of terrestrial stars in the stone wall made their target perfectly clear. An area not more than five feet across, and a little below the middle of the height of the wall. That, Ginger said with certainty, was where the bulge was. And if anything was going to shatter Colin Barron, short of a thunderbolt from heaven, it was the whole wall at his left shoulder exploding on top of him.

"Is it time?" whispered Ginger, still captain of this venture, but without a watch.

"Now!" said Willie the Twig softly, and they all braced their arms firmly in the frame of the ladder, and leaned forward for the word.

"Charge!" croaked Ginger, and the whole half-dozen, eyes fixed unrelentingly on the area of stars, launched themselves forward in a vehement, unsteady trot, instinctively feeling for a rhythm, lurched into the double, gathered breath and accelerated into full, triumphant gallop many yards from the target.

It was something out of another world, mad and marvellous and exhilarating in its desperation, something that happens only once in a lifetime. Toby thought of all those short legs twinkling behind him, and all those enlarged hearts pumping adrenalin like crazy, enough to flood the old fish-ponds and overflow into the river.

The twin poles of the ladder hit the target dead-centre, with six translated personalities for motor. The check was merely momentary, no more than a slight jolt, before the points sheered on with only slightly retarded momentum, exploding into the light beyond in an avalanche of flying stones. Through a quivering, quaking gap three yards wide the victorious team with their battering-ram burst into Bossie's prison. From the doorway George Felse, Sergeant Moon and two or three constables, closely followed by Barbara Rainbow, exultant, with streaming hair, surged in to meet them.

Through a stifling acrid dust-storm, thick as old-fashioned fog, George dived headlong for Colin Barron's half-buried body, and fell on his knees to dig like a terrier at the litter of stones and rubble that covered him. Praise God, at the instant of total, deafening shock he had done the instinctive thing, dropped his captive to throw up both arms to cover his head. Not too successfully; there was blood as well as dirt in the thick fair hair, and he was stunned, but the damage looked relatively trivial. Concussion, probably, but no fractures. Like so many of the mediaeval walls that look so irreproachably solid, this one had been rubble-filled within the stone shell. But the point of impact had been barely six feet from his left ear, and the heavier ammunition had sprayed at that level, and effectively knocked him out. Bossie, held closely in front of him and shielded by his body, was somewhere there underneath, and with any luck no worse than winded.

George on one side and Moon on the other were still scooping away debris and lifting Barron's weight aside, as Willie the Twig and Toby Malcolm came clambering in recklessly through the gap they had made, four dusty choirboys-errant hard on their heels, and all in a state of awe and exaltation at the wreckage they had produced, and total euphoria at its successful result. Minor avalanches still slid and muttered along the wall, where a tattered area of sky appeared, its shape changed every few seconds by the belated fall of one more precariously balanced stone. Coughing and spitting out gritty particles, they plunged enthusiastically into the work of rescue.

Thankfully they extracted Bossie, temporarily winded but without much more than a scratch on him, unwound him from rope and gag, retrieved his glasses unbroken, cleaned them, and stood him on his feet, as good as new. Doubtless he should have been in a state of nervous collapse, but there were no signs of it. As soon as he had any breath, he was as voluble as ever.

"Aren't you going to put handcuffs on him?" he demanded, surveying his prostrate enemy. "It is him! He's the one I saw the night Mr Rainbow was killed. When he locked the door I saw the light flash off that flat stone in his ring, and I remembered it. And I bet he's got my parchment on him, too."

Reaction might come later, but Bossie was Bossie yet, and not to be swept away immediately into Jenny's arms, not before his vindication was complete. It was, in any case, an idea that was worth considering. With so great a cloud of witnesses, less than half of them police, just as well to lift the evidence on the spot, if it really was there, before any question of its provenance could arise.

The contents of Colin Barron's pockets were without special interest, until they came to a deep breast-pocket inside his jacket, and drew forth something rolled up like an oversize stick of cinnamon inside a narrow suede bag.

"That was Arthur's," said Barbara immediately. "He had a set of those made once, when he'd got hold of some very special Georgian silver cutlery, and wanted to carry samples to show. I doubt if there'd be others exactly like them."

Out of the case slid a rolled, brownish tube faintly marked with traces of faded ink. Unrolled, it also displayed clearly enough the fresh characters of Bossie's effort, far too positive to be convincing for long.

"Yes," said Bossie triumphantly. "That's it!" Who should know his own handiwork better?

"That's the thing I pinched," agreed Toby. "Plus my friend's improvements, of course."

Several pairs of eyes peered at the unprepossessing relic, between puzzlement and awe, willing to be impressed but unable to see any sane reason why they should be.

"You mean," enquired Spuggy wonderingly, "*that*'s what it was all about? Just that bit of old stuff? Is it that precious?"

"Two people evidently thought so," said George soberly.

"Well, how about this, then?" And Spuggy fished in the depths of his own overcrowded pockets, and produced a longish, flat wad of what looked like disintegrating plaster, and on the surface, indeed, was nothing else. "It's that piece I poked out when we went round this afternoon," he explained simply. "It seemed to make that chap so mad I'd thought I'd better not leave it lying around, so I slipped it in my pocket. But all the plaster bits started flaking off, and I found this other stuff folded up inside. Look!"

No need to exhort them, they were all looking, with disbelieving eyes, as he thumbed apart the edges of not one, but apparently three or four leaves of something that might very well be vellum. Stiff, inclined to crumble, but very slowly unfolding now to show remarkably clear edges of inner surface, preserved by being pressed together. There were certainly the marks of written characters there, the opening letters of line below even line. Gritty particles of mortar drifted from it as Spuggy held it up to view. "It looks like some of the same. And Bossie said it was where the other bit was found. Is this any good?"

For a moment nobody had breath to answer him.

"Because if it is," continued Spuggy practically, "there's some more of it down here among all this muck. I reckon it came down with the wall."

As one they turned to stare, and then scattered to peer and rake and dig all along the broken area of wall, among the ruin of the north walk, where once the carrels and aumbries of Mottisham Abbey had been ranged, and the monks had both read and written. And first one excited voice, and then another, hailed fresh discoveries. Wherever the wall had weathered and fallen into holes, it seemed, the leaves of parchment had been rolled or folded and wedged into the cracks as filling, to be plastered over and seal the gaps. In the days of penury and decline, when repairs were impossible, something had to stop the holes to keep the wind away! The treasure for which Rainbow had died and Colin Barron had killed lay scattered in dust and rubble at their feet.

11

THERE was precious little sleep for anyone connected with the Mottisham affair that night. Even when Bossie had been restored to parents limp with reaction, but just resilient enough to receive him back with deflationary calm, even when Sergeant Moon and Willie the Twig had ferried all the victorious choirboys back to the bosoms of their families, with flattering accounts of their ingenuity and heroism, calculated to inflame parental pride and disarm parental rage, even when an ambulance had carried away a conscious but incoherent Colin Barron to hospital and strict guard, pending a charge of murder, and a flustered John Stubbs had arrived to complain bitterly about the wanton damage to his wall, the activity within the north walk of the cloister still continued. So momentous a find demanded a police guard until it could be taken over by the proper authorities, and a call after midnight to Charles Goddard, and another to Robert Macsen-Martel, had brought both gentlemen hurrying to view the unexpected windfall. Its value would not be assessed for a long time yet, and even its ownership might produce some problems, though none that could not be agreeably resolved, for the future endowment of the abbey was a cause dear to all the parties concerned.

Bossie, as voluble as ever, abruptly fell asleep almost in mid-sentence on the way home, and was carried to bed, sunk so deep out of the world that he never roused when they undressed him, sponged him clean of the dust of his adventures, and inserted him into his pyjamas. Jenny had qualms that this might be the sleep of withdrawal, and his awakening next day a recoil into horror, but Bossie rose fresh as a daisy after his short night, and headed for school with a purposeful gleam in his eye, and an epic tale to tell, which would lose nothing in the telling. There was still a faint pink line round his neck, but he seemed quite unaware of it. He went off eagerly to catch the bus, and left two very thoughtful people gazing after him.

"He doesn't seem to have been really afraid at all!" said Jenny, both appalled and reassured. "How is it possible?"

"Must be a question of faith," suggested Sam. "I suppose he really has imbibed a kind of religious certainty that the righteous must prevail."

"Good God!" whispered Jenny. "Have we really prepared him as badly as all that for the world he's entering?"

"Or as well?" wondered Sam, after astonished thought. "It hasn't done so badly by him up to now, has it?"

★ ★ ★

After twelve days of intensive police business, George finally found time to pay a visit to Abbot's Bale again, and look up all the interested parties. It was Sunday evening once more, and he took time out to attend the evening service at St Eata's. The churchyard was reconsecrated by then, cleansed of the relatively innocent blood, and the trebles of the choir lifted up their earnest faces and angelic voices in a Stainer anthem, with Bossie soaring serenely into the stratosphere in a brief solo, and afterwards, during one of the Reverend Stephen's more incoherent but disarming sermons, towed a small pink sugar mouse with a candlewick tail, courtesy of Toffee Bill, the length of the *cantoris* side on a nylon thread, while on the *decani* side they were busy composing one of the best of their hymn-line quatrains;

'When shrivelling like a parchéd scroll.
Far from my home on life's rough
    way,
Why restless, why cast down, my soul?
Timor mortis conturbat me!'

Miss de la Pole was nodding gently in her pew, apparently well content with the way things were being conducted after her retirement. In the organ loft Evan Joyce let loose the peals of glory with immense Welsh hwyl, and all the tunes were the time-honoured best of tunes, so that the congregation could enjoy themselves, as was only right and proper in worship. In fact, all seemed to be very well with Abbot's Bale and

St Eata's church and parish.

Afterwards the Reverend Stephen, slightly shamefaced but smiling, showed George the sheet of paper the *decani* trebles had been circulating.

"Actually, I collect them, but they don't know that, of course. They always mean to pocket them, and usually forget, I've got quite a number. Considering everything that's happened, there's something psychologically profound about this one, wouldn't you say? 'When shrivelling like a parchéd scroll . . .' That's Spuggy, you know. Who would believe such a line could be found in Ancient and Modern? From parchéd scroll to parchment isn't far, you'll agree. And then that last one — that was Bossie, of course. None of the others would have known it, and strictly speaking it's cheating, because it isn't in the hymnal, though maybe it ought to be. And in any case, the last-liner is allowed to use his imagination if he can't come up with a real line. Do you suppose this is his inmost self speaking? It certainly isn't any other part of him, it's incredible any child could ride such an experience with such complete phlegm."

"I think," said George, "it's just his love of sonorous Latin coming out naturally. I doubt if he's ever applied it to himself."

"I hope not. Or that if he ever did, he's already forgotten it. Of course he is bossier than ever, but that's also natural. No doubt he'll get his come-uppance some more subtle way, sooner or later."

* * *

What Jenny said was: "I never sat still for so long in my life. Do you think it will be counted to me for an acquisition of merit? I could have murdered him myself when I got him back, but I never so much as scolded."

George thought it well to turn her mind away from what was over. "Have you heard from Toby? He's going to be wanted at the trial, unless we get a guilty plea, which I very much doubt, though he did make some pretty damaging admissions at first. I expect he'll take them all back."

"Toby's at Worcester just now. Thespis raked in such a haul at Comerbourne, because of the publicity, they're getting almost famous in their small way. Bookings even for next year! I'll tell him you were asking, he said he'd keep in constant touch."

"Give him my love," said George, "and tell him to be good!"

★ ★ ★

His last call was far up the valley, and aside from the narrowing road that climbed over into Wales. The mixed forest closed over him gently, like cupped hands folding him in, spiced with conifers and airy with deciduous trees, well-laced with undergrowth below, and teeming with untroubled night-life, the primitive paradise ruled over by Willie Swayne. At the lodge George parked the car, and Barbara came round the corner of the log house to see who had driven in, Barbara in dungarees and sweater, both clearly the property of Willie the Twig. Her hair was loose about her in a raven cloud, and her face was as clear and radiant as a star. The two lissom red setters hugged her on either flank, and were jostled on the right by a fallow fawn, silvery and dun in the headlights, with huge eyes that wondered at him but were not afraid.

"She's only young, this year's. Her mother got injured and had to be shot when Amanda was only a baby. She's in love with Willie, he's going to have trouble convincing her she's a fallow doe. I should blame her?"

The exquisite creature danced away happily among the trees with the two dogs, her natural enemies, when Barbara haled her visitor into the house. In a very few miles Barbara had come a long, long way. The lodge was hectic, chaotic and primitive, there had been no attempt to impose order on Willie the Twig's bachelor housekeeping. It was also comfortable, warm, wood-scented and intimate. Two people inhabited it, but innumerable friends, four-footed, winged, shy and secret, came to visit, confident of their welcome.

"Then it really is going to turn out to be something momentous," marvelled Willie, dispensing drinks. "And no dealer gets the money value out of it, after all."

"Seems to be a matter for amicable negotiation between Macsen-Martel, the Trust and the Department how the value's going to be realised and what will be done with it. But nobody's grabbing for himself. Presumably it will be used to maintain the abbey. Not that anyone has any idea what its value is as yet."

"But what exactly is it?" asked Barbara. "The whole of the abbey library, walled up there for safety? Did they hide them that way to save them, when the place was due to be plundered?"

"Not a chance! Not rolled up and stuffed into holes, like that. No, the general opinion seems to be that by that time they were a tatterdemalion lot, without much Latin between the handful of them, and such was the surviving respect for learning, they just used their books for stopping when the wall fell into disrepair. But the irony is, of course, that by doing so they did preserve them — from possible destruction at the Dissolution, and from time and weathering and dispersal ever since. It's going to take them weeks to take down the whole wall, as they have to now, and months, maybe years, to clean and recondition and sort all the fragments, but by what they've found already, it's going to be worth it."

Evan Joyce, doubly blessed, was taking part in the decyphering of those first texts. Bossie would undoubtedly claim a look-in as often as possible, and his fair share of the credit.

"Nobody knows what it's going to add up to by the end, but they've already reclaimed bits of the abbey accounts from round about fourteen hundred, and what's exciting them much more, some passages from what seems to be a thorough-going historical chronicle, as detailed as Matthew Paris or St Albans, and about the same time. More than one hand, the original chronicler probably had continuers later. One more independent window on the Middle Ages. The sort of thing that will end as a treasure of one of the main national libraries, and be consulted by scholars for ever after."

"Instead of going to some private collector for a big price," said Barbara, "probably abroad."

Yes, it might well have been like

that, whether Rainbow had succeeded in running it to earth, or Colin Barron had stolen it from the thief in his turn.

"He admits to having been on the tower with your husband that night. I think his defence is going to be that the fall was accidental, but it won't stand up. I think he tried to get cut into the deal, and when he got nowhere, was certain he was on to a fortune, and felt he had an opportunity too good to miss. Silence, and night, and no witnesses. I think by then he had a fair idea of what your husband was carrying. Something acquired at choir practice — you remember? — and something that sent him hunting in the tower among the papers in the chest there . . . He knew it when he found it on the body, and he could do enough with it to connect it with the abbey, but I suspect Bossie's particular interest in that wall was what made him turn his attention there, after he'd volunteered to do the rounds, and had the place to himself. Or thought he had!"

"But I don't understand," said Barbara, grave in recollection, "how Arthur ever came to let himself be inveigled to the top of the tower. Colin followed him up to where the chests were, yes, but what brought them out on to the leads?"

"I think by that time it had already gone beyond discussion, and come to menaces. And Barron was younger, bigger, and between him and the way down. There was only one way to go. And time gained is time gained. Someone might have walked in below, something might have happened to scare the threat away. But nothing did. Evan Joyce had repented of his own curiosity and gone home, thinking no evil. There was only Bossie, down in the churchyard. Five minutes more, and he'd have gone home, too, and there'd have been no witnesses and very little evidence."

Barbara sat cross-legged on the rug in front of the fire, her hands pensively clasped in her lap, and one of the setters stretched out beside her with his head on her thigh. She was silent and thoughtful for some moments before she pronounced the considered epitaph of Arthur Rainbow.

"He wasn't a bad person. In a way I liked him, and when he made a bargain, written or not, he kept it. I don't complain of him. But though I never wished him any harm, I can't be sad. And the really sad thing is that I don't suppose there's a single other person who can, either."

They both went out to the car with him. The autumn night smelled of timber, fir-needles, moist fallen leaves, and the faint hint of frost. The dogs roused when Willie roused, and padded attentively at heel. The fallow fawn came out of the trees like a silver wraith, slender and silent. No, Barbara could hardly be expected to be sad.

"Let me know when the wedding date's fixed," said George at parting.

"Wedding?" said Willie the Twig, as though confronted by a conception rather surprising and totally irrelevant, as indeed it probably was. But on second thoughts he appeared to be finding some merit in the idea, even if it was no more than a decorative flourish to something that already existed and was guaranteed in perpetuity. "Yes," he said thoughtfully,

"I suppose we might get round to it in time."

"I rather fancy having Amanda attend me up the aisle," agreed Barbara. "And we could find a nice solo for Bossie among the hymns. That would probably be the day his voice broke, and he did a belly-flop from a high C into a terrifying baritone."

"That," said Willie the Twig, "would be just right for our wedding, and I should enjoy it. But it won't happen. You should know by now, that kid always falls on his feet."

THE END

TO FIGHT THE WILD
Rod Ansell and Rachel Percy

Lost in uncharted Australian bush, Rod Ansell survived by hunting and trapping wild animals, improvising shelter and using all the bushman's skills he knew.

COROMANDEL
Pat Barr

India in the 1830s is a hot, uncomfortable place, where the East India Company still rules. Amelia and her new husband find themselves caught up in the animosities which seethe between the old order and the new.

THE SMALL PARTY
Lillian Beckwith

A frightening journey to safety begins for Ruth and her small party as their island is caught up in the dangers of armed insurrection.

THE WILDERNESS WALK
Sheila Bishop

Stifling unpleasant memories of a misbegotten romance in Cleave with Lord Francis Aubrey, Lavinia goes on holiday there with her sister. The two women are thrust into a romantic intrigue involving none other than Lord Francis.

THE RELUCTANT GUEST
Rosalind Brett

Ann Calvert went to spend a month on a South African farm with Theo Borland and his sister. They both proved to be different from her first idea of them, and there was Storr Peterson — the most disturbing man she had ever met.

ONE ENCHANTED SUMMER
Anne Tedlock Brooks

A tale of mystery and romance and a girl who found both during one enchanted summer.

CLOUD OVER MALVERTON
Nancy Buckingham

Dulcie soon realises that something is seriously wrong at Malverton, and when violence strikes she is horrified to find herself under suspicion of murder.

AFTER THOUGHTS
Max Bygraves

The Cockney entertainer tells stories of his East End childhood, of his RAF days, and his post-war showbusiness successes and friendships with fellow comedians.

MOONLIGHT
AND MARCH ROSES
D. Y. Cameron

Lynn's search to trace a missing girl takes her to Spain, where she meets Clive Hendon. While untangling the situation, she untangles her emotions and decides on her own future.

NURSE ALICE IN LOVE
Theresa Charles

Accepting the post of nurse to little Fernie Sherrod, Alice Everton could not guess at the romance, suspense and danger which lay ahead at the Sherrod's isolated estate.

POIROT INVESTIGATES
Agatha Christie

Two things bind these eleven stories together — the brilliance and uncanny skill of the diminutive Belgian detective, and the stupidity of his Watson-like partner, Captain Hastings.

LET LOOSE THE TIGERS
Josephine Cox

Queenie promised to find the long-lost son of the frail, elderly murderess, Hannah Jason. But her enquiries threatened to unlock the cage where crucial secrets had long been held captive.